"It seems I arrived
just in time!"

Ruel approached Julie standing at the steps. The young man she'd been with had vanished, but badly as her date had behaved, Julie was determined to stand her ground.

"Perhaps you'll be more selective in choosing your dates in future," Ruel went on. "Beachboys are rarely satisfied with just kisses."

His arrogant attitude triggered her temper. "What about you?" she challenged. "You had a date tonight. Were you satisfied with just kisses?"

The glitter in Ruel's eyes mocked her. "We weren't discussing my personal affairs, Miss Lancaster. But I think I'm beginning to understand you. Whether you're willing to admit it or not, you've wondered what it would be like if I kissed you."

"That isn't true!" Julie denied hotly. But it was true and she knew it.

JANET DAILEY AMERICANA

KONA WINDS

Harlequin Books

TORONTO • NEW YORK • LONDON
AMSTERDAM • PARIS • SYDNEY • HAMBURG
STOCKHOLM • ATHENS • TOKYO • MILAN

The state flower depicted on the cover of this book is
hibiscus.

Janet Dailey Americana edition published November 1986
Second printing May 1988
Third printing May 1989
Fourth printing May 1990
Fifth printing July 1991

ISBN 373-89861-4

Harlequin Presents edition published January 1980
Second printing February 1982

Original hardcover edition published in 1979
by Mills & Boon Limited

CHAPTER ONE

THE CAR TIRES crunched over the narrow, snow-packed street emptied of traffic by the late midnight hour. Warm air blasted from the heating vents inside the car, but it couldn't hold back the invading cold from outside.

"Brrr! I wish I were back in sunny California." Julie Lancaster clenched her teeth to keep them from chattering.

"It's only the first of January. Winter has just begun," warned Marilyn Stuart, who was driving.

"Don't remind me!" Julie snuggled deeper in her heavy parka and moved her chilled feet in a more direct line to the heating vent blowing on the floorboards.

A native Californian, Julie had lived in the Boston area for the past five and a half years. The company her father worked for had transferred him here just before the start of her senior year in high school. At the time, Julie had vowed that as soon as she had graduated she was returning to California to attend college, but a certain young man had changed her mind. That romance waned into nothing her first year in the Boston college. After that, other considerations kept her there—mostly the increased financial burden of transferring to a California college where she couldn't live at home and where tuition costs would be higher.

"Home sweet home," Marilyn announced as the car rolled to an idling stop at the curb.

Julie's mouth gaped in a tired yawn that she couldn't stifle. Her back and legs protested their weary soreness when she attempted to move. "I don't know whether to soak my feet or just fall into bed," she sighed. Almost eight straight hours of standing and walking had made her feet feel like two swollen, throbbing appendages at the end of her legs.

"At least the tips were good tonight," her fellow worker consoled.

The way Julie felt, she had earned every penny of the money in her uniform pocket, but she didn't say so. "Thanks for the ride home, Marilyn." Her hand hesitated on the door handle. Tired as she was, there was a matter that Julie had intended to discuss with Marilyn, but she had forgotten it until this moment. "Listen, if you're going to keep chauffeuring me back and forth from the restaurant, we're going to have to come to some kind of agreement about the gasoline."

"Your place is on my way home," her co-worker said shrugging.

"Maybe so, but it's worth something to me not to have to stand out in the cold waiting for a bus," Julie argued.

"We'll talk about it." Marilyn postponed the discussion to another time.

Julie was so tired that she let her. "Good night." She pushed the door open and stepped onto the shoveled walkway to the house.

Despite the teaching degree she had, Julie hadn't

been able to obtain a position in her chosen field. While her good looks and easygoing manner were assets as a waitress, they had proven to be a hindrance when she applied for teaching posts. All her life, Julie had wanted to teach American history at the high school level. Her interviewers had all expressed grave doubts about her ability to control a classroom when she didn't look older than her students, but without experience, she hadn't been able to disprove the doubts. It was a depressing circle.

The one bright spot was the substitute teaching post she had with one of the Boston public schools. Through it, she hoped to gain the needed experience, but so far, the teachers had been disgustingly healthy and minus any family emergencies. Only twice had Julie been called in. She wouldn't have obtained that post if it hadn't been for the strong recommendation she had received from the parents of a teenaged girl she had privately tutored.

In the meantime, she supported herself by working nights as a waitress. It practically eliminated her social life, but she was usually too tired to be overly concerned about that.

The house was dark as she approached, except for a flickering square of light coming through the sheer curtains of the front window. She inserted the house key in the lock, turned it and pushed the door open. Standing in the doorway, she turned and waved to Marilyn who had waited at the curb to make sure she had got safely into the house.

Over the low rumble of the car's engine as Marilyn drove away could be heard the sound of a televi-

sion discoursing its late-night fare of old movies. It
was the same greeting Julie always heard when she
entered the closed-off entryway with its staircase to
the second floor. She glanced at the door where the
sound was coming from and the corners of her wide
mouth lifted briefly. Mrs. Kelly, her landlady, was
addicted to television, especially the late, late movies.

A month after Julie had received her college di-
ploma, her father had been transferred again, this
time to Florida. She could have gone with her parents, but she had decided it was time she were whol-
ly independent. In June of this past year, she had
rented the apartment from Mrs. Kelly, which con-
sisted of one large room with a bath.

The second floor of the old house had been con-
verted into three rooms to let. Because of her working hours, Julie knew her fellow lodgers only by
sight. Both worked during the day, which precluded
much opportunity of forming close friendships. The
two other women seemed nice, but Julie didn't know
either of them well.

With a last glance at the front door to be sure the
night lock was bolted, she moved to the stairs. The
second step creaked under her weight. Before she
reached the third step, a door opened and Humphrey Bogart's voice was clearly recognizable from
the television sound coming from the room.

"Julie—it is you. I thought I heard the door,"
Mrs. Kelly declared in a very Bostonian accent.

"I'm sorry, Mrs. Kelly, I didn't mean to disturb
you." Julie paused on the stairs.

Her landlady was in her sixties, widowed, with an abundance of pearl-gray hair piled in a bun on top of her head. Typically it was askew. Mrs. Kelly claimed to be five feet tall, but Julie doubted it. With the added height advantage of the staircase, she thought that the older woman looked even shorter. There was something about the woman that reminded Julie of a leprechaun. Maybe it was the constant twinkling in her eyes.

"You didn't disturb me." Mrs. Kelly waved the apology aside. "I've been listening for you."

"You have?" Julie murmured inadequately, hoping her landlady wasn't going to invite her in to share some hot chocolate. Julie had accepted such invitations in the past, but tonight she was just too tired.

"Yes, you had a telephone call shortly after you left for work this afternoon. The woman said it was very important. Just a minute and I'll get it for you. I wrote it all down on the paper beside the telephone." The small form disappeared into the room lighted only by the television tube.

A telephone call that was important. Obviously it wasn't from her parents, since Mrs. Kelly had met both of her parents and taken calls from them. That left one possibility, the school. They wanted her to teach tomorrow. Julie leaned tiredly against the stairwell wall. If that were the case, she desperately needed some rest. It would ruin everything to arrive at the classroom in the morning groggy from lack of sleep.

"Here it is." Mrs. Kelly reappeared, waving a piece of paper in her hand.

"Thank you." Julie descended two steps to reach the paper in the outstretched hand. The light in the stairwell wasn't good. Neither was Mrs. Kelly's handwriting. She didn't attempt to decipher it there. "Good night, Mrs. Kelly."

"Good night." The door was closed and Humphrey Bogart was muffled into an unidentifiable voice.

In her room, Julie switched on the overhead light and bolted the door. Unbuttoning her coat, she read the note. A Mrs. Grayson wanted her to call first thing in the morning—the telephone number was written below the message. Julie couldn't remember any Mrs. Grayson with the school. It took her tired mind several seconds to place the name. It was the woman from the professional employment agency. Julie had signed up with them last summer in hopes that they would be able to obtain her a teaching post in a private all-girls school.

After all this time she had given up hope. Maybe they had finally arranged a job interview for her. Releasing a sigh, Julie draped her coat over the back of a chair. She hadn't the energy to get excited by the possibility. Tomorrow morning would be soon enough.

Sitting on the same chair that held her coat, she untied her shoes and slipped them off, curling her toes and rubbing her aching arches. Her peripheral vision caught a glimpse of her reflection in the wall mirror. Straggly wisps of hair had escaped from her schoolmarmish bun at the nape of her neck. Julie didn't attempt to smooth the strays into place. Instead she unpinned the coil and shook her straight hair free.

Its color was not exactly light brown, neither was it dark blond, but fell somewhere in between. The California sun had usually bleached it to an unusual and attractive shade of platinum gilded blond. Since she had moved east, it had become an indistinguishable color. Tan was the closest descriptive word Julie knew, but who had ever heard of tan hair? Straight and sleek, it framed her oval face from a center part, its indefinite color accenting the pale brown of her eyes.

At the moment, her eyes were too tired to inspect her reflection and take note of the quiet beauty of her features that blossomed into loveliness under the golden kiss of the sun. Sighing, she rose. The bed looked singularly inviting, more so than a soak in the tub, no matter how sore and tired her muscles were. Her movements were automatic as she undressed and got ready for bed.

The small apartment was sparsely furnished. A single bed and a chest of drawers joined a narrow drop leaf table with two chairs as furniture. Half of one wall was taken up by makeshift wooden cabinets, a tiny gas stove, and a small refrigerator. The starkness of the furnishings was alleviated by the colorful poppy-designed cloth covering the table and a coordinating reddish orange spread on the bed. Lemon and lime toss pillows mounded the bed.

An assortment of sunny posters and appliquéd

cloth pictures brightened the sun-yellow walls; the
woodwork was painted a pristine white. Even the
enamel of the refrigerator and stove were decorated
with magnetized ornaments, from butterflies to
ladybirds, and bright pot holders. The entire room
was a touch of sunny California in winter Massachu-
setts. But, as Julie piled the pillows onto the floor
and swept back the bedspread, she didn't notice the
cheerfulness of the room. Sleep was the only thing
on her mind.

The next morning she used Mrs. Kelly's telephone to call Mrs. Grayson at the employment
agency. Fully rested, she was intensely curious, but
Mrs. Grayson seemed reluctant to satisfy her curiosity over the telephone.

"Do you have a job interview for me?" Julie asked
the point-blank question after Mrs. Grayson had
asked her to come to the private employment agency.

"I do have a job offer for you," the woman stated
without any qualification. "I would like you to come
in so we can discuss it."

"A job offer?" Julie repeated. It sounded too good
to be true. "Teaching?"

"Yes, teaching," Mrs. Grayson assured her.
"What time can you come to my office? Please try
to make it as soon as possible."

"I'll leave now."

Julie splurged and called a taxi. She had been
offered a job—teaching! Only now did she admit the
fear she had been hiding—that she would be like so
many college graduates who could not find a posi-

tion in their chosen field. Not even the post as a substitute teacher had given her much encouragement for a future, permanent position.

By the time she had seated herself in Mrs. Grayson's office, she was so excited that she had difficulty retaining her composure. Her attempts to appear cool and calm were betrayed by the sparkling in her eyes.

"You were going to tell me about this job offer." She came straight to the point.

"Yes." Mrs. Grayson sifted through the papers on her desk and withdrew one halfway down a stack. "I received a telephone call yesterday afternoon from a Miss Harmon. She wants to hire you to tutor her niece. She has offered a——"

"Tutoring?" Julie repeated in disappointment. "I thought you said it was a teaching post."

"Tutoring is teaching," the woman reasoned. "Besides, I think you'll find this offer very attractive."

"Perhaps." But Julie felt misled. She couldn't summon much enthusiasm for it.

"You see, Miss Harmon and her niece live in Hawaii." A faint smile edged Mrs. Grayson's mouth at Julie's startled glance. "I thought that might get your attention."

"How did she know about me?" Dazed, Julie tried to recall whether or not Mrs. Grayson had actually said she had been requested for the job. She was certain she had.

"Do you remember the Rifkins? You tutored their daughter this past summer. You were highly recommended to Miss Harmon by them," was the explanation. "Now Miss Harmon is most anxious to engage you."

"But surely there's someone in Hawaii she could hire for her niece," Julie insisted.

"I'm certain there must be," Mrs. Grayson agreed. "I didn't inquire why Miss Harmon specifically wanted you, other than to learn about the recommendation she'd received from the Rifkins. I can only presume she's indulging in a whim of the wealthy. Importing a tutor from Boston is probably something of a status symbol that she's acquiring."

"I see." It sounded logical in an illogical way.

"Would you like to hear more of the particulars?"

"Yes, of course." She would be foolish not to.

"Miss Harmon's niece was injured in an automobile accident shortly before the Christmas holidays, as I understand. It's anticipated that her injuries and recovery are going to keep her out of school possibly for the balance of this school year. The girl is sixteen, a junior in high school, and most anxious to graduate next year with her classmates."

"So the position would be for roughly five months," said Julie, roughly calculating the length of the school year that remained.

"Miss Harmon has guaranteed six months' salary to persuade you to leave whatever teaching post you're now holding." Mrs. Grayson smiled with a slight hint of conspiracy, and named a salary figure that dazzled Julie. More and more, it was becoming an offer she couldn't refuse—not that she had contemplated refusal.

"You will live with Miss Harmon and her niece. Miss Harmon also wanted me to assure you that a nurse had been hired and you would not be required to do any sickroom care. Evenings and weekends you would be totally free to do as you please."

"It sounds too good to be true—a paid vacation in Hawaii in the dead of winter!" A faint laugh escaped Julie's throat as she shook her head in amazement. "Where do I sign? When do they want me?"

"Immediately."

"But my job——"

"Miss Harmon is paying a high price for your services as well as taking care of our agency's fee. Naturally she expects you to come when it's convenient for her. I have a first-class plane ticket for you here, paid for by Miss Harmon, with the reservation for the day after tomorrow. I'm to telephone her this afternoon to confirm that you've accepted her offer and will be on that plane."

"The day after tomorrow. That isn't much time," Julie murmured, thinking of all the washing and packing she had to do, not to mention informing the restaurant and school that she was quitting without notice.

"What's your answer?"

"What else can I say?" Her shoulders lifted in an expressive shrug. "Yes. Tell Miss Harmon, yes."

A few minutes later, she rose to leave, with the address of her new, if temporary, place of residence in Hawaii, an unpronounceable town on the island of Oahu. She still felt a bit dazed by her good fortune.

Mrs. Grayson rose to see her out. "Send us a postcard to let us know how you're getting along, Julie."

"I will," she promised.

"*Aloha.* I believe it means 'goodbye' and also 'good luck.' "

"Thank you. *Aloha,*" Julie returned the Hawaiian greeting and a smile curved the full width of her mouth.

Outside, she succeded in flagging down a taxi for the ride back to her apartment. Bundled up in her winter parka, a wool scarf around her throat, she gazed out of the window at the bleak, gray skies and snow-packed streets. In two more days she would be looking at palm trees and sandy beaches. It seemed impossible.

Mrs. Kelly was at the door to meet her when she arrived. "Did you get the job?"

"Yes." Her head bobbed in an eager response. Julie pulled off her mittens; she was bursting with the news. "Mrs. Kelly, it's in Hawaii!"

The bright blue eyes widened expressively. "Hawaii!"

"Yes, can you believe it? I have to leave the day after tomorrow." The information was barely out when Julie realized, "That's hardly enough notice for you to find someone to rent my apartment, but I'll pay you a month's rent." All the things she had to do and all the arrangements she had to make began crowding into her mind. "I won't be able to take all my things in the apartment. I'll need a place to store them. Would you have room somewhere? It would probably be just a couple of boxes."

"Of course I have room. I have the whole downstairs," the landlady declared.

"I'll gladly pay you for keeping them," Julie assured her quickly.

"Gracious, no! I've always dreamed of going to Hawaii. If you'd send me some postcards and maybe some little souvenir, that would be payment enough. Remember Dorothy Lamour in her sarong, dancing the hula?" Mrs. Kelly waved her arms out to the side and attempted to make her hips sway in the native dance.

"I'll send you dozens of postcards," Julie promised as she shrugged out of her heavy coat. "Oh, before I forget, I have the address where I'll be living so you can forward my mail to me."

"Let me write it down." The landlady took the slip of paper Julie had retrieved from her purse and walked into the living room. "Will you be moving to Hawaii permanently?"

"I don't know. I hadn't thought about it." Not until this moment. Perhaps if she succeeded in impressing this Miss Harmon with her competency as a teacher, the woman would recommend her for a position in the local school system. Miss Harmon seemed to be a woman of apparent wealth, and probably influence.

"Since you have a job there, I would certainly live there for a while if I were you," Mrs. Kelly stated, bending over a pad and copying the address.

"The job is only temporary. I'm tutoring a young girl who's been injured in an automobile accident," Julie clarified her position.

"Oh, you're going to be a governess." The landlady straightened.

"Not exactly. The girl will be returning to school as soon as she's able. I'll be following the curriculum set by the school she regularly attends, so it isn't quite the same," Julie explained. "And since the job isn't permanent, I don't know if I'll be staying on there. It will depend on whether or not I can find another position."

"You're an intelligent and attractive young woman. I'm sure you'll find something." Mrs. Kelly returned the original slip of paper with the address on it to Julie.

"I hope so. But right now, I have to start getting organized. I have to call the school and Joe at the restaurant."

"Don't forget to call your parents."

"Yes, I'll do that tonight when both of them will be home. Don't let me forget, Mrs. Kelly," she added.

"I won't," the woman promised.

"I'll need some boxes for all my dishes and linen." Julie began listing the things she had to do. "I'll have to pack my clothes and put away all my heavy winter things—I won't be needing them in Hawaii. Heavens, I have clothes to wash!" A whole basketful, she remembered.

"You bring your dirty clothes downstairs to me. I'll wash them for you," Mrs. Kelly offered.

"Would you? You are a darling, Mrs. Kelly. I'm going to miss you." Julie gave the diminutive female a quick hug. "I'll bring the clothes down right now."

With her purse and heavy parka clutched in her arms, she took the steps two at a time to the second floor. Below she could hear Mrs. Kelly singing some old melody and caught the words "heavenly flower." Julie knew she would be much too busy in the next thirty-six hours to do much singing, but Mrs. Kelly was doing it for her. There were such a staggering number of things to accomplish before she left.

CHAPTER TWO

"LADIES AND GENTLEMEN, we are making our descent for Honolulu International Airport." The pilot's voice came over the intercom. "The weather in Honolulu is seventy-two degrees, overcast skies, with occasional light showers. Despite the inclement conditions, those of you on the right side of the aircraft should have an excellent view of Diamondhead and the Waikiki beach when we break through the clouds."

In her right window seat, Julie leaned closer to the curved glass. The sleek jumbo jet was engulfed in a cloud, a gray white world outside its windows. Although she was exhausted from the frantic schedule of the past forty-eight hours, including more than eight hours of flying, Julie was determined not to miss her first glimpse of the island of Oahu.

The cloud dissipated into wispy trails and then nothing. Etched against the oyster-gray backdrop of the overcast was the familiar bulk of Diamondhead jutting into the sea. Directly below, the Pacific Ocean churned up whitecaps, sending rows of foaming white to the shore. A jungle of building blocks rose behind the pale strip of beach—the mass of skyscraper hotels and offices portraying a city in miniature. Houses climbed the slopes of the mountains behind the beach as the city of Honolulu seemed to tumble over itself in search of room. It was a city much larger than Julie had expected.

The No Smoking sign flashed on and a stewardess announced that they were making their final approach for landing. Julie leaned back in her seat and refastened her belt. A curious anticipation of what was before her chased away the tiredness, not just for the job, but for the people and the place. The aircraft wheels seemed to thud onto the runway and seconds later the powerful thrust of the jet engines reversed itself. The plane slowed to taxi to the terminal.

Having a first-class ticket gave Julie the advantage of being one of the first to leave the aircraft. She emerged from the long tunnel of the jetway into a glassed boarding concourse. The instructions from Mrs. Grayson had said she would be met at the airport, but they hadn't included the information of where and by whom? Julie took a deep breath and walked forward, unconsciously scanning the small group of people waiting at the gate, as if she would recognize someone.

"Miss Julie Lancaster! Miss Julie Lancaster!"

She heard her name being paged by a male voice in the group. Other names and tour groups were being called, and it took her a minute to identify who was seeking her. The voice belonged to a Hawaiian man who looked like he was in his late thirties, of medium height with a waistline that had begun to thicken. His hair was as jet black as his eyes.

"I'm Julie Lancaster," she told him.

The friendly smile that enveloped his face was

easy to return. "*Aloha,* Miss Lancaster." He took the *lei* he held and placed it around her neck. In the same motion he lightly kissed her cheek. "Welcome to Hawaii."

Like his smile, the kiss on her cheek had been totally friendly. Julie wondered if this was an example of the "*aloha*" spirit that she had heard came so naturally to the islanders. She touched a finger to the pale yellow petal of one of the tubular flowers strung one after another into the *lei.* The blossoms' spicy fragrance reminded her of ginger. She guessed that that was what the flowers were.

"Thank you." She meant the words sincerely.

"In Hawaii, we say *mahalo,*" the man smiled again, warmth and gentleness radiating from his face.

"*Mahalo,*" Julie repeated.

"You're welcome." The dark head bobbed in acceptance of her gratitude. "This way, please. Miss Emily is waiting for you over here."

Miss Emily? Julie supposed he meant her employer Miss Harmon and followed him. Standing to one side of an exit was a fairly tall and very erect woman. A naturally colored straw hat was on her head, the white band around the crown almost matching the woman's hair. She wore a navy blue suit, the skirt covering her knees and sensible navy blue shoes. The cotton blouse beneath the navy blue suit jacket was buttoned all the way to the throat. Julie gained the overall impression of someone starched and prim. She didn't feel nervous about meeting her employer, only curious.

"Miss Lancaster, I'm Emily Harmon." The older woman greeted her with a smile that, while it wasn't as all encompassing as the man's had been, was friendly.

"How do you do, Miss Harmon." This time Julie was greeted with the more traditional firm handshake. "And thank you for the *lei*. It's lovely."

"We couldn't overlook the Hawaiian custom of greeting *malihinis*."

"Newcomers, tourists," the man defined the term.

"Dan has the car waiting outside," Emily Harmon announced. "Dan is actually our mechanic. He only doubles as a chauffeur when I have to come into Honolulu. I can't stand the traffic and the congestion."

Julie found herself being escorted out the exit door. "My luggage," she offered in faint protest, aware of the stream of passengers heading for the baggage area.

"Give your claim tickets to Dan. He'll collect your luggage for you," the woman commanded, and Julie obeyed. A silver-gray Mercedes was parked not far from the door. As they walked toward it, the woman issued another order. "Breathe in. Tell me what you smell."

Julie did as she was told again. There was an elusive quality to the air she breathed, something soft and gentle, but she couldn't identify it. The alert blue eyes of Emily Harmon read her expression.

"It's clean air," she explained. "It's been washed by thousands of miles of ocean, kept cool by the water while acquiring the softness of rain. That first breath will be indelibly etched on your memory."

Julie's lips parted in astonishment that the explanation could be as simple as clean air. "It's wonderful!" she exclaimed.

"Yes, isn't it?" Emily Harmon returned, a trifle smugly. Dan held the rear door of the Mercedes open for them. Julie climbed in first, sliding to the far side behind the driver. When Emily Harmon was safely inside, Dan closed the door. "He's going to drive around to the baggage claim area," Emily explained as if to reassure Julie that they weren't leaving without her luggage.

"Of course," she nodded.

"Were you able to see Honolulu and Waikiki when you landed?" the older woman questioned.

"Yes, I did, and Diamondhead, too."

"What did you think?" It wasn't an idle question; Emily Harmon was interested in her reaction. Dan was behind the wheel; the engine purred into action.

"It's a much larger city than I imagined, and there were a lot more skyscrapers than I thought there would be," Julie admitted.

"My family once had a beach house on Waikiki. That was when the only hotel was the Royal Hawaiian. It's difficult to believe, isn't it? Of course, that was long before the war. Now there are so many hotels all up and down the beach that the Royal Hawaiian is practically lost in their shadows. Ruel says it's progress."

"I suppose so." Julie wondered who Ruel was. It

was an unusual name. But she didn't have a chance
to ask as her employer continued.

"You'd be surprised at how many tourists come
here, stay on Waikiki for a week and believe they've
seen Hawaii. They go home with their Hawaiian
shirts and a crate of pineapples and become an instant authority on Hawaii." She paused for a considering moment. "When Captain Cook landed here,
he called the chain the Sandwich Isles after his spon-
sor the Earl of Sandwich. Did you know that?"

"No," Julie admitted.

"Then the whalers came and the missionaries.
When I sée those people on the beach wearing those
ridiculous pieces of cloth called bikinis, I find it
difficult to believe that my forebears taught the Hawaiians to put *on* clothes." The woman's biting wit
reached out to charm Julie, grooving a smile in the
corners of her mouth.

The car rolled to a quiet stop in front of the baggage area and Dan stepped out. "Don't be too long
in there, Dan," Emily Harmon admonished. "I
don't want to arrive home too much after dark."

"Yes, Miss Emily."

With the instruction given, the woman returned
her attention to Julie. "You have an unusual accent,
Julie. May I call you Julie?"

It was a question that demanded an answer.
"Please do," she gave permission.

"What part of New England are you from? My
ancestors came from New England. They were
among the early missionaries here."

Looking at the proper and fastidious Emily Harmon, Julie found it easy to believe that. "Actually, I'm not from New England. I was born and raised in California, although I attended college in Boston."

"Oh." There was a wealth of meaning in the simple word. Julie was positive she had just fallen several notches in Emily Harmon's esteem. "I was under the impression you were New England born."

"I'm sorry, no. Does it matter?" Julie couldn't resist asking.

"No, not really, I suppose," the woman sighed regretfully. "It's just that New England people tend to be more reserved and controlled, less exuberant if you will. I felt Deborah needed someone of that type just now."

"Deborah is your niece?"

"Yes, She's such an active, outgoing person that her confinement during recovery is going to be a problem. I had hoped for someone who would project a calming influence." Emily Harmon looked thoughtful. "Perhaps, though, your youthfulness will provide her with some companionship."

"How old is she?" asked Julie.

"Sixteen. She'll be seventeen in March. How old are you?"

"Twenty-two."

"So young!"

Julie dropped another notch in the woman's estimation. "I graduated from high school when I was only seventeen," she explained.

"You do seem mature and levelheaded."

Julie was positive that Emily Harmon had mentally tacked on the qualification—even if you are from California. She swallowed the smile that was teasing her mouth and decided to shift the subject.

"I know Deborah was in an automobile accident. How badly injured was she?"

"We expect a full recovery, no permanent injuries. She's in a body cast—for a broken pelvis, among other things. I won't bore you with the gory details. As I told your Mrs. Grayson, we have a nurse staying with us, and she'll see to all of Deborah's physical needs. Ah, here's Dan with your luggage." She spied the stout Hawaiian approaching the Mercedes. "We'll soon be home."

"How far do you live from here?" Julie asked.

"It's about an hour's drive. We live near the north shore, one of the last bastions on Oahu against 'progress.' " There was disdain in the sweeping look Emily Harmon gave the buses and taxis and automobiles zipping in and out of the terminal complex.

When Julie's luggage was stowed in the trunk of the car, Dan slid behind the wheel and drove the sleek car off the airport grounds into the mainstream of traffic. Within minutes he entered a modern freeway system, complete with bumper-to-bumper traffic three lanes wide. The skies were still overcast and were darkening to slate with the approach of a hidden sunset.

"I've made an appointment for you to meet Deborah's teacher late tomorrow afternoon after classes," Emily told her. "After traveling all day today and adjusting to the time zone change, I know you'll need to sleep late in the morning."

"That's thoughtful of you," Julie acknowledged. "I am tired, but I'm sure a good night's rest will be all I need." She hesitated. "I was wondering about Deborah's parents. I had the impression from Mrs. Grayson that they'd died."

Emily leaned forward and tapped Dan on the shoulder. "You're speeding!"

The car slowed perceptibly under her reprimand and Emily Harmon watched until she saw the speedometer register the legal limit before she sat back in her seat. Julie's glance caught Dan's gaze in the rearview mirror and he winked. The gesture seemed to say that he and Emily Harmon were constantly at odds over the pace he drove.

"About Deborah's parents," the woman returned to the question Julie had asked, "they were both lost at sea when she was five. They'd gone sailing, when there was a sudden squall. The coastguard found the wreckage of their boat on a reef a couple of days later."

The tight line of the woman's mouth indicated that she found the subject painful even after all this time. Julie decided against pursuing it any farther. She began studying the road signs and was confronted with a mass of unpronounceable words—Wàipahu, Aiea, Wahiawa, Wailua, Haleiwa, Waianae. Her tongue couldn't seem to roll over all those vowels.

"Are those names of towns?" She pointed to a sign.

"Waipahu and Waianae—yes, they are." Emily Harmon pronounced them effortlessly.

"I'll never be able to pronounce them," Julie laughed a trifle self-consciously.

"It can be a bit confusing at first. The Hawaiian language only consists of seven consonants—*w, p, h, l, k, m,* and *n*—and the five vowels. With only twelve letters, we make use of them all. I believe we have a beginner's Hawaiian grammar book in our library. Remind me to give it to you."

"I'm sure I'll need it," Julie sighed.

Within minutes after the car had climbed away from the coast onto a broad, flat plateau flanked by two mountain ranges they became encased in darkness. The headlights illuminated little of the open country on either side of the road. The freeway system ended at the town of Wahiawa.

As they drove past a U.S. Army base, Emily Harmon identified it. "That's Schofield Barracks. When the Japanese attacked Pearl Harbor, they made their first strike here, bombing and strafing the base."

"I didn't realize it was so far inland," commented Julie.

"Most people don't. They think it was somehow adjacent to the naval base at Pearl Harbor, which, of course, it isn't." As they passed the last entrance gate to the base, the car was again in darkness, the lights of the town left behind.

"As I mentioned to your Mrs. Grayson," Emily Harmon continued, "your evenings and your weekends are your free time. You're a young and an attractive woman and it's only natural that while you're here, you're going to seek some male company. I wouldn't presume to dictate what you should do or whom you should see on your free time. However, I feel obligated to issue a word of caution. We have a lot of military personnel stationed on this island, plus many surfers on the north shore. Most of these young men are interested in only one thing from girls, and that's sex."

Julie was surprised by the bluntness of the statement. For all her prim and starched appearance, Emily Harmon said what she meant. Julie smiled, knowing she was going to like this woman.

"That's what most of the young men back in the States are interested in, too," she offered dryly.

"The mainland—always refer to the other forty-nine States as the mainland. Hawaii is in the United States. We *kamaainas* are a bit touchy about that. So, if you don't want to offend us, use the term mainland," Emily Harmon instructed.

"A *kamaaina* is a native or an old-timer," Dan explained.

"You watch the road, and slow down!" The order was issued sharply to the driver. More calmly, she turned to Julie, her tone becoming once more quiet and reasonable. "Now, as I was saying, I wouldn't presume to dictate to you, but I think it would be wise to screen your choice of escorts to try and save yourself any hurt or embarrassment."

"I do appreciate your word of caution, and I'll keep it in mind," Julie promised. She found her employer's concern to be slightly touching. She suspected that it had to be genuine since she didn't see how any indiscretion on her part could cast a bad light on Miss Harmon's good name.

Conversation lapsed for the rest of the drive. Julie felt the accumulated tiredness of the last two days drowning her. She fought to stay awake and not become mesmerized by the inky black world outside the windows of the luxury car. The car passed through another small community and paralleled the shoreline of the ocean for a while. A couple of times, Julie glimpsed the almost iridescent white of the swelling ocean waves rushing to shore. Finally Dan took a turn onto a side road, taking the Mercedes up a switchback onto a tree-lined lane.

"Here we are," Emily Harmon declared unnecessarily when Dan stopped in the circular drive.

Lights gleamed a welcome from the windows. I was too dark for Julie to see many details of th outside of the house. Trees seemed to hover about i to keep it hidden and secluded. It was white and two story, and gave the impression of being large. Dan was there to open the door and assist her out of the car. Then he performed the same service for his employer.

The front door of the house was opened before Julie and Emily Harmon had climbed the short flight of steps to the wide veranda. Again Julie found herself looking into a friendly Hawaiian face, only this time it belonged to a female in her forties, still trim and attractive.

"Julie, this is Malia. She takes care of us," Emily Harmon introduced. "Malia, this is Julie Lancaster."

"*Aloha*," the woman smiled.

"*Aloha*." Julie found it amazingly natural to return the same greeting.

The white walls of the interior added to the feeling of spaciousness. The large entryway was furnished with white wicker furniture covered with bright green cushions to continue the tropical theme of the numerous potted and hanging plants that adorned the large room. The atmosphere suggested that the rest of the house was equally spacious and casually elegant, but, more important, warm and inviting. At the far end of the room, a staircase of a light polished wood climbed in a series of three tiers to the second floor.

"I've fixed a light snack, if you would like?" the woman named Malia offered.

"No, thank you," Julie refused. "I had more than enough to eat on the plane."

"I think Julie would like to be shown to her room," stated Emily Harmon. "After traveling all day, I'm sure she would prefer to bathe and have an early night."

"I would, yes," Julie admitted.

"I generally have breakfast at nine o'clock on the *lanai*. If you're awake at that time, perhaps you would like to join me," her employer invited.

"I would like to, thank you."

"I'll show you to your room," said Malia in her soft, melodic voice. "Dan will bring your luggage up shortly."

"Good night, Julie," Emily Harmon wished her.

"Good night," she returned. "I'll see you in the morning."

"Sleep as late as you wish," the older woman insisted, and moved away to an open archway.

Julie followed Malia up the staircase, silently admiring the innate grace of the woman's carriage. At the head of the stairs, the woman turned to the right down a windowed hallway. At the second door she stopped and opened it. Walking into the room, she turned on a switch to flood the room with light, and Julie entered to find a room with the same white walls that predominated in the house.

This one was offset by a bold and attractive combination of coral and sunny yellow. The unusual color combination was in the quilted spread on the bed and repeated in the full-length curtains and the area rug on the floor. Besides the bed, dresser, and a chest of drawers, there was a writing desk and chair, and a small divan, its thick plush cushions covered in a shiny print that incorporated the two colors with a dark green.

"It's a beautiful room," Julie declared.

"Your private bath is through this door." Malia showed her, then walked to the curtains, pulling them apart to expose latticed, French doors, paneled with sheers. With a flick of a wrist she opened them and stepped aside as Julie came forward.

As she stepped into the warm night air, Julie saw that the balcony ran the full length of the house, the roof reaching out to shelter it. It overlooked a swimming pool, its shape barely discernible in the flickering light of two flame torches. Beyond were shrubbery and more trees.

"My very own balcony!" It seemed like a dream. It lacked only a moon and a canopy of stars.

Julie turned to share the delight she felt with Malia, but Dan had entered the bedroom with her luggage, and Malia was telling him where to set it. Julie put aside her pleasure for the business at hand and returned to the bedroom closing the doors.

"*Aloha ahiahi*," Dan smiled to Julie as he withdrew from the room.

Uncertain how to respond to that, Julie simply nodded and smiled. When the door closed, she turned to Malia, unable to keep the puzzled look out of her pale brown eyes. One corner of her mouth lifted in a confused smile.

"What did he say?"

"It means 'good evening,' " Malia explained with a beaming and understanding smile. "Now you just show me which of these bags has your night things and I'll unpack it for you while you bathe."

"No, you don't need to do that," Julie refused. "I can take care of it."

"Of course you can, but I'm going to. Now you tell me which one and go relax in the tub."

"No, please, I can't let you. Besides, maybe Miss Harmon will want you for something," Julie argued.

"No, Miss Emily knows there's a cold tray of food on the table and her tea is hot on the warmer." Sparkling black eyes surveyed Julie. "Now, you're tired—you've got circles under your eyes. You go take that bath and tell me which of these suitcases has your night things, otherwise I'll open every one of them."

Julie knew when she had been defeated by a superior force and pointed to the small weekend case. "But you leave the rest of the unpacking to me. I work here, too, Malia." A thought occurred to her. "I should have met Deborah tonight, but I was so tired that I never thought about it."

"Debbie will understand. She's a good girl."

Running a hand over the carved headboard of the bed, Julie began wandering about her private student. Was she spoiled? Wilful? Filled with self-pity? Wouldn't it be awful if she were chained to a know-it-all little bitch for five months or more?

"What's she like, Malia?" She studied the woman's face as she answered.

"She's a wonderful girl—happy, generous. She loves everybody!" The light that had been shining in her expression faded as Malia sighed and lifted the suitcase onto the bed. "That's why it hurts so to see her lying in that bed."

"She was in a car accident," Julie prompted.

"Yes. Debbie and some of her friends went to a rock concert in Honolulu. They were on their way home when some car tried to pass another car on a curve. They nearly crashed head-on, but the boy who was driving swerved into a ditch."

"Were any of the others in the car hurt?"

"One had a broken leg and another a broken arm. Otherwise, it was just cuts and bruises. Debbie was the one who was the most seriously hurt. Luckily all the doctors have said there isn't any permanent damage. It's just going to take a long time for her to heal and——" Malia glanced up just as Julie yawned. She hadn't meant to be rude, but she was so tired she couldn't help it. "Go take your bath before you fall asleep leaning against the bed."

"I guess you're right," Julie conceded. As she straightened from the bed, the *lei* around her neck brushed her chin. "What about my *lei*? Do you suppose it will keep?"

"Ginger? No, they're very short-lived." Malia shook her head slightly.

"Oh, well," Julie sighed in resignation and took the *lei* from around her neck to drape it over the bedpost.

A half an hour later, when she slipped beneath the covers, bathed, refreshed, and tired, the spicy fragrance of the blossoms scented the air she breathed. As she closed her eyes, she decided it was an excellent way to go to sleep on her first night in Hawaii.

CHAPTER THREE

JULIE AWOKE EARLY the next morning. Of course, by Boston time, it was late. She shrugged away the time zone difference and fluffed her long hair one last time with the brush. The radio clock on the dresser indicated 8:35. Her employer had said to join her for breakfast at nine on the *lanai*.

Smiling at her reflection, she murmured, "But I forgot to ask what or where is a *lanai.*"

With a characteristic shrug, she walked out of the door into the hallway. There was bound to be someone around the house who could point her in the right direction. If not, she'd find it somehow.

Rain beat against the windowpanes in the corridor. Hawaii was anything but sunny today, she observed. She peered out one of the windows, but could see little but the sheets of rain. She decided that she much preferred it to snow and sleet.

Her shoes made little sound on the stairs, their rubber soles treading quietly on the steps. With two tiers behind her, she turned down the last one. At the sound of male voices approaching the large entryway at the base of the stairs, her foot hovered on the next step. She glanced up as two men entered the area from another part of the house. One of the men was tall, towering over the second shorter and broader man. It was the tall one that caught Julie's interest.

His hair had the color and sheen of rich mahogany, growing thickly to his collar. The white material
of his shirt was stretched across the set of his broad
shoulders, then tapered to the trim waistband of his
dark trousers. He looked remarkably fit—in excellent physical condition.

The shorter of the two men spoke. "Ain't no work
to do on a day like dis. Dem Kona winds are bad,"
he said in an enchanting kind of local Pidgin English.

"Yes, I know, Al. Those Kona winds never bring
anything good." As if sensing a third party was
listening to the conversation, the tall man made a
leisurely turn and looked directly at Julie.

Even though she had been caught accidentally
eavesdropping, there wasn't a shy self-conscious
bone in her body. Since her presence had been noticed, she continued her descent of the steps. The
white of her slacks gave her a long and leggy look.
Her lemon-yellow pullover top had three white
bands at the waistline, which completed the outfit.

"Maybe dem Kona winds will blow all away by
tomorrow," the shorter man commented.

"Maybe. I hope so, Al." His gaze never left Julie.

"I'll be goin' now. See ya tomorrow."

"Right."

Now that the man faced her, Julie could see his
masculine features were hard and vital, browned by
long hours of exposure to a tropical sun. A pair of
arresting blue eyes were making a cool and thorough
appraisal of her. The line of his mouth held no gen-

tleness but contained an abundance of cynicism. It didn't curve into a smile as she approached.

"You are Julie Lancaster," he identified her without hesitation.

But it was only logical, she decided. After all, she was the one who was the stranger in his house. Immediately, she wondered why she had reached the conclusion that he lived there. Was it his superior attitude?

Taking his lead of not issuing a formal greeting, she replied, "Yes, that's right. I'm afraid you have the advantage. You know who I am, but I don't know who you are." She softened the challenge with a smile.

"I'm Ruel Chandler."

The unusual name clicked in her memory. Emily Harmon had mentioned it yesterday at the airport. Despite his lack of friendliness, this Ruel Chandler intrigued her. The fascination she felt must have registered in her look, because she noticed the shrewd and knowing gleam that glinted in his eyes.

"I'm pleased to meet you, Mr. Chandler." Her head bobbed in a demure nod. She wondered what his position was in the house. "You are . . . . " She hesitated deliberately so he would fill in the blank.

"I'm Debbie's brother," he stated, vague amusement in his voice.

Julie didn't have to feign surprise. "Oh. I didn't know Debbie had a brother. Her name is Chandler?"

"Yes."

"Then Emily Harmon is——"

"My mother's sister."

"I had it all mixed-up. I never bothered to ask. I simply presumed that Debbie's last name was the same as your aunt's. I should have asked."

"It doesn't matter." Not a single expression seemed to crack the hard set of his features, but Julie thought she detected a note of boredom.

In another minute he might walk away and she would still be lost. "Perhaps you could help me. I have a small problem," she said.

"What is it?" He tipped his head to the side, vaguely indifferent.

"Your aunt asked me to join her for breakfast this morning on the *lanai*. My problem is I don't know where or what a *lanai* is." Julie smiled at her own ignorance.

"It's a porch or a balcony. Emily usually has her breakfast on the *lanai* on the ground floor," he explained with seeming patience. A hand gestured toward the rain darkening the windows. "But, as you can see, it really isn't the kind of weather to be eating outdoors today. Breakfast will be served in the dining room. It's right through that archway." He pointed in the direction from which he had just come. "You can't miss it."

"Thank you." Her gratitude was met by a dismissing nod before he moved off in another direction. She watched him for a couple of seconds, then walked through the archway he had indicated. A living room led into a dining room where Emily Harmon was seated.

"Ah, Julie." She glanced up. "Did you have a good night's rest?"

"Yes, I did, thank you."

"Sit wherever you like," Emily instructed. "What will you have? Juice? Fresh fruit? Pineapple? Papaya? Malia will fix you some eggs."

"I'll just have some fruit and toast. I've never been able to eat a large breakfast," Julie took the chair at the table opposite from her employer.

"Pineapple or papaya?" Malia inquired.

"I believe I'll try some papaya."

As Malia disappeared through a door, Emily offered, "Coffee?"

"Yes, please, black." Julie noticed a place setting at the head of the table. It hadn't been used. She supposed it was for Ruel Chandler.

Malia returned carrying half of a papaya in a bowl, a green tinge to its ripely yellow skin. It was a melonlike fruit of a rich orange color. A lemon wedge was in its hollowed-out center.

"Squeeze the juice over the fruit," Emily Harmon instructed. "It tones down the sweetness and gives it a tangy flavor."

After following the suggestion, Julie scooped out a spoonful of the fruit. It was delicious, tangy but sweet. Emily was waiting for her opinion.

"It's very good," Julie assured her.

"Malia, why don't you go see if Ruel is going to join us this morning? I'm not even sure if he's up yet. I know it was very late when he came in last night," her employer stated.

"He's up." Julie offered the information, and was

immediately the recipient of Emily's questioning gaze. "I met him in the entryway just before I came in. He was talking to someone named Al."

"You met him, then?" It wasn't exactly a question.

"Yes, he introduced himself." Julie laughed shortly. "I wasn't aware that Debbie had a brother until he told me."

"Never mind going after him, Malia. If he's going to join us, he'll be along. He probably went to see Deborah," Emily decided.

"Very well." Malia glanced at Julie. "I'll bring you some toast."

"Actually Ruel is Deborah's half brother," Emily offered the information as the housekeeper left the room. Her voice was very matter-of-fact. "Deborah is the daughter of Ruel's father's second wife."

"Oh," Julie digested that for an instant. "Then you aren't really related to Debbie."

"Not by blood, but I consider that an unimportant detail."

And Julie believed her. Emily Harmon seemed genuinely devoted to the young girl Julie had not yet met. "What does Ruel do?" she asked.

"He manages this place and he has business interests in Honolulu and Waikiki." The last was admitted very grudgingly.

The statement Emily had made yesterday at the airport about Ruel came back to Julie. She had been talking about the tall string of hotels and skyscrapers and said that Ruel called it progress. Julie knew that was a touchy subject with her employer, so she avoided it.

"It was too dark last night for me to see much and with the rain this morning, I really don't know all of what you have here," she commented.

"Sugar fields mostly and Ruel runs cattle in the hills," came the information. "Of course, he spends most of his time in Honolulu with his other . . . projects. Al oversees most of the work around here." The tone of her voice left little doubt that it was a situation Emily Harmon didn't like.

When Malia returned with the toast, Julie let the conversation lag. Ruel and his activities seemed to be a sore issue with Emily. She thought it was best to let the subject fade out of the woman's mind before attempting to discuss anything else.

After breakfast was finished, Emily suggested, "Let me take you to meet Deborah so the two of you can become acquainted."

Julie agreed readily to the proposal and the two of them left the dining room. Rain continued to come down outside, but it wasn't the deluge it had been. The air in the house was muggy and warm.

"Deborah's room is here on the ground floor. It used to be Ruel's bedroom, so his comings and goings at odd hours wouldn't disturb the rest of us. After Deborah's accident, it was much easier to move his things to a guest room on the second floor than to try to get a hospital bed upstairs. Plus—" a smile briefly touched the woman's mouth "—when Deborah does begin perambulating, we won't have to worry about her falling down the stairs!"

They were crossing the entryway and Julie glanced at the U-shaped stairwell and understood Emily's concern. Not only would it have been difficult to cart a bulky hospital bed up and around those steps, but also dangerous for anyone on crutches to negotiate the polished wooden treads of the stairs.

Entering the smaller, second wing of the house, they passed a room that was a combination study and library. The door stood open to reveal an unoccupied room. A second door was also open. It was this one Emily entered.

The room was dominated by the stark serviceability of a large hospital bed. A dark-haired, dark-eyed girl lay framed by the white sheet. Julie felt the warmth in the girl's smile and was reassured that Malia hadn't overexaggerated her praises last night.

"Hi, Auntie Em," Debbie Chandler greeted her aunt first, but the interest of her gaze was centered on Julie.

"I brought Miss Lancaster in to meet you," her aunt explained unnecessarily, and turned to Julie. "This is my niece, Deborah Chandler."

"How do you do, Miss Lancaster. I hope you had a good flight over here."

Julie approached the bed. "I did, thank you, although it was a long one." One side of the girl's face was faintly discolored, but the bruises had practically faded. "And please, call me Julie."

Keeping up the formality of "Miss" on a one-to-one basis would be difficult under any circumstances, but the natural openness of this girl would have made it doubly so. Julie decided to dispense with it from the beginning.

"This is Sue Ling, my nurse," Debbie made the introduction of the slim Oriental woman, uniformed in a white pant suit, as she lifted a tray from a service cart.

"Glad to have you with us, Julie," the nurse smiled.

Again Julie felt thoroughly welcomed. "I'm glad to be here." Of all the people she had met since she arrived, only Ruel Chandler had held himself aloof. But it was foolish to think about him. He wasn't the reason she was here. The girl in the hospital bed was.

"I'm glad to have you here, too, Julie," Debbie offered. "My right arm and my head are the only two things that aren't plastered, in traction or otherwise immobilized. I need to put them to use."

"I'm going to do that all right," Julie laughed. How many people could joke about their condition, especially sixteen-year-olds? Perhaps it was the resiliency of youth. "I'll probably turn out to be such a slave driver that you'll be glad to get back to school."

"She's nice, Auntie Em," Debbie declared. "Thank you for bringing her over."

"I'm glad, Deborah." Emily Harmon's face softened with unbelievable tenderness. "I'll leave you two alone now. I have some other work to do."

"I'll take the breakfast tray back to the kitchen. I won't be long." Sue Ling made her exit from the room with the older woman.

"Ruel told me he met you this morning," said Debbie.

"Yes, I was lost. I had to ask him for directions," Julie admitted, making light of the matter.

"I know. He told me," was the smiling response. Julie could just imagine what he had told her—your new teacher didn't know what a *lanai* was. "What did you think of him?" Debbie asked eagerly, and Julie was at a loss as to how to answer the question. But evidently an answer wasn't required. "All my girl friends think he's quite a hunk of man. They practically melt whenever he's around."

"He is handsome." The edges of Julie's wide mouth twitched with a smile. She couldn't help wondering what Ruel Chandler's reaction was to this teenage adulation his sister implied.

"He isn't really handsome. He's just so . . . virile," the girl settled on the adjective after a searching pause. Then she smiled at herself. "As you can tell, I think he's pretty great, too."

"I know what you mean. I have an older brother, too. He's pretty special to me." Julie chose a safe response.

"You do?"

"Yes. He's married now, and he and his wife have two little girls. I haven't seen him in quite a while. They live in Michigan," Julie elaborated.

"We have something in common."

"I guess we do, Deborah," Julie smiled.

Laughter sparkled in the dark eyes. "Call me Debbie—Deborah sounds so sophisticated. Aunt

Em indulges in wishful thinking when she calls me that!"

"Debbie it is, then."

"What's your favorite subject?" The girl seemed determined to find something else in common with her new teacher.

"American history."

"Mine's English. What about maths?"

"It's my weak spot," Julie admitted.

"Mine, too."

"We both might be in trouble, then!"

They talked for a while longer. Julie kept the conversation centered on Debbie's schoolwork, finding out what she had learned and what interested her. All the information she would obtain later that day from Debbie's teacher, but she wanted to get a feel of her pupil's reaction to learning. The vibrations were very positive.

When Sue Ling came back, Julie used it as an excuse to leave. "I haven't unpacked my suitcases yet, so I guess I'd better get started. I'll talk to you later, Debbie."

It was still raining when it came time to keep the appointment with Debbie's schoolteacher. Emily Harmon accompanied Julie, although she didn't take part in her discussion with the teacher. Julie couldn't make up her mind whether her employer was merely being polite or wanted to observe how knowledgeable Julie was with a fellow professional. Either way, Julie felt she had acquitted herself admirably and returned to the house with an armload of books, school records, and subject study schedules.

"We have dinner promptly at seven," Emily told her on their arrival at the house. "I generally change but it isn't required for you to do so. And I have no objections at all if you choose to wear slacks to the table."

Julie decided that since it was her first dinner, she should wear at least a nice skirt and blouse. Besides, the clothes she had on were damp from dashing in and out of the rain. Wearing an ocher gold skirt and a matching print blouse of silk, she came downstairs shortly before seven, and joined her employer in the living room. There was no sign of Ruel Chandler.

Promptly at seven, Emily rose from her chair. "Shall we go in to dinner?"

"But," Julie hesitated, "aren't you going to wait for your . . . nephew?"

"He knows what time we have dinner. If he isn't here, we start without him," was the uncompromising answer.

"With the rain and all, he might be delayed by the weather." Julie didn't understand why she felt she had to make excuses for him.

"I've learned to expect Ruel when he arrives," Emily explained. "At thirty-five, he's much too old to be answering to me about his comings and goings."

"Does he drive to and from Honolulu every day?" Julie was curious.

"Practically." Emily Harmon led the way into the dining room.

"That must be tiring."

"He keeps an apartment in the city. If it's too late, he simply stays there."

Somehow Julie doubted that he always spent the night alone. She glanced around the dining room, so comfortable and elegant with its rich woods and glassed doorway, to the courtyard and swimming pool outside. Ruel Chandler not only had all the comforts of home, but a bachelor pad as well. He had his cake and was eating it, too.

Emily Harmon had noticed Julie's gaze stray outdoors. "I quite often have my evening meal on the *lanai*, especially if both Ruel and Deborah are away." Her lips thinned. "I hope this Kona weather doesn't last long."

"It has something to do with the winds, doesn't it?" asked Julie.

"The tradewinds come from the northeast. They're our predominant winds," her employer explained, "coming along with fair skies and sunshine. When the winds are from the south, it means rain and high humidity. No one likes to see the Kona winds come."

"Why are they called Kona winds?" That was the part Julie didn't understand.

"They take their name from the big island of Hawaii and its Kona coast. Since the big island lies south of Oahu, the winds coming from that direction are also coming from Kona, hence Kona winds."

Malia came in with the soup course and the discussion of the weather was put aside. Fresh fruit and cheese were served for dessert. Ruel Chandler still had not made an appearance. They had tea in the living room while Malia cleared the dining table.

"I think I'll go see Debbie," said Julie when she had finished her tea. "Do you mind?"

Emily Harmon glanced up from the magazine she was reading. "No, go right ahead."

The portable television set in the bedroom was on when Julie walked in. Debbie seemed surprised to see her, but the surprise quickly gave way to pleasure.

"Are you ready to hit the books tomorrow?" Julie asked half-teasingly.

"As ready as I'll ever be."

"What are you watching?" She glanced at the screen as a commercial flashed on.

"Nothing. At least, nothing that's interesting." There was boredom in the faint sigh the girl expelled.

"I noticed this morning that you had quite a record collection." Julie wandered over to the turntable and the rack of albums in the stand beneath it.

"They're mostly rock," Debbie offered in warning.

Sending a smiling look over her shoulder, Julie asked, "Is there any other kind?"

The smile was broadly returned. "According to Auntie Em, there is. Sue Ling isn't crazy about it, either. Why don't you pick out a couple of albums and put them on?"

Julie did, then sat cross-legged in a chair by Debbie's bed. They talked for a while, about music and anything and everything. Julie found more to like in the girl. At times she seemed oddly mature; other moments she was innocent and vulnerable, totally without guile. In all respects, she was a typical teen-ager, interested in music, boys, school, and the future.

The second album was half through when the telephone rang. It was on the stand by Debbie's bed, within reach of her uninjured right arm. Julie could tell that it was one of Debbie's girl friends and guessed the conversation would sooner or later get to a personal and private level of teenage confidences.

"I'll see you in the morning," she whispered as she uncoiled her legs from the chair.

"You don't have to go, Julie," Debbie protested. "It's only Cathy, one of my girl friends."

"You don't really want your teacher listening in on your conversation," Julie insisted with a knowing smile. Debbie started to argue, before nodding an admission with a rueful grin. "Good night, Debbie."

"Good night."

When Julie didn't find Emily Harmon in the living room, she went on upstairs to her bedroom. She went over the work sheet she had drawn up for the next day's subjects and went to bed shortly after ten. To her knowledge, Ruel Chandler hadn't arrived home.

CHAPTER FOUR

DURING HER FIRST WEEK, Ruel Chandler only had dinner with them twice. He was pleasant and courteous to Julie, but he didn't go out of his way to make her feel a part of the family. His attitude was such a contrast to everyone else's that she sometimes let it bother her. Wanting everybody to like her had always been one of her faults. So she tried to ignore the frustration she felt.

Her first free weekend she decided against doing any sight-seeing. She would have time enough to tour the whole island in the next few months. Wearing a swimming suit beneath her slacks and blouse, she thought she would get a bit of sun and do some souvenir shopping for her friends and family. Emily suggested that she could accomplish both in the small town of Haleiwa and offered to loan her one of the economy cars. But Julie decided to go by bus, even though it meant a long walk down the switchback road to the highway.

Haleiwa was a quaint village with its old storefronts and roadside fruit and shell stands. A small shopping center, recently erected, maintained the rustic motif of the older stores, complete with board sidewalks. It was a peaceful seaside community.

After exploring a general store and a neighborhood art gallery, she lunched outdoors at a sandwich shop. Then she wandered down to the small harbor.

With the protection of a sunscreen, she lay out for a couple of hours in the sun and watched the sailing boats and cruisers going in and out. Later she returned to the town proper, purchased some souvenirs and caught the bus back.

Having been walking almost all day, she found the road leading to the house seemed much longer, plus she had the added burden of the purchases she'd made. She began to wish she had accepted Emily's loan of a car as she eyed the steep switchback road to the upper plateau.

A car roared toward her from behind and Julie moved to the grassy shoulder. Instead of swerving past her, it slowed to a stop beside her. At first glance she saw only the sleek, black sports car with the passenger door opening before she finally recognized Ruel Chandler behind the wheel.

"Hop in," he ordered smoothly.

With the daunting prospect of climbing that hill, Julie didn't need a second invitation. "Thanks." She slid into the bucket seat, juggled her packages, and closed the door.

Immediately the car was shifted into gear and it shot forward. "Been shopping, I see." His blue gaze flicked to the assortment of bags on her lap.

"I've been into Haleiwa," she offered in explanation.

"Nothing more ambitious than that?" He sounded as if he were mocking her, but Julie couldn't be sure. She was determined not to let his condescending attitude get under her skin.

"Nothing more ambitious than that," she returned the phrase as a statement. "Not this weekend." The low-slung car seemed to snake around the tight curves up the hill. "I thought I'd go to the beach tomorrow, swim, just take it easy."

"If it's swimming and sun you want, you're better off making use of the pool at the house," he told her. "We have some very strong currents here on the north shore and powerful undertows, not to mention coral reefs that are as sharp as razors. The beach at Haleiwa or Waimea Bay is about the only place for what you have in mind. If there aren't any breakers, you can feel safe swimming at Waimea."

"I'll remember that, thank you." She accepted his advice. Within seconds he was braking the car to a stop in the circular drive of the house. "Thanks for the lift, too. It would have been a long hard walk." She was determined to be pleasant and properly but not overly appreciative.

"It was no trouble."

Leaving the car parked in the drive, Ruel walked up to the house with her and opened the door, since her hands were full of packages.

"Thanks again." Julie smiled. The acknowledging nod of his head was courteous and nothing more as he returned to the car.

"Ruel?" Debbie called from her bedroom.

"It's me—Julie."

"You're back already!" came the loud reply.

It was silly to keep shouting back and forth. Julie walked to the girl's bedroom and appeared in the doorway before answering. "I'm back already."

"You certainly have an armload of souvenirs

there," Debbie observed. "Did you find anything for your landlady?"

"I think so." Julie set her packages on a chair and opened one. She had mentioned to Debbie about Mrs. Kelly, her penchant for old movies and her Hollywood idea of Hawaii. "Do you suppose she'll like this?"

From the bag, she shook out a *muu-muu*. The flowered material was predominantly scarlet with a splash of orange and yellow. She held it up in front of her for Debbie to see.

"The color is all wrong. Much too bright," Ruel commented from the doorway.

Julie pivoted correcting quickly, "It isn't for me."

"It's for her landlady, Mrs. Kelly," Debbie added.

"Do you hate her that much?" A brow lifted in mocking inquiry.

"No," Julie denied that and glanced at the audaciously bold material. "I think this is what she would expect."

"Yes," Debbie agreed. "It's exactly the kind of thing Dorothy Lamour would wear," she said and giggled.

Ruel glanced from one to the other. "This must be a private joke."

It was, and Julie didn't feel like explaining it to him. She folded the long dress and returned it to its bag. Immediately she began gathering the rest of her packages as Debbie responded to his comment.

"It is kind of a private joke, but you might not appreciate the humor." With amazing tact, Debbie changed the subject. "I thought I heard your car drive in just before Julie arrived."

"I did. I gave her a ride from the highway."

"At least you didn't have to climb our miniature Matterhorn," Debbie teased.

"That's what I thought," Julie agreed with the sentiment. "I'll take these things upstairs to my room. Talk to you later, Debbie."

"Okay."

Ruel stepped to one side to let Julie past. The touch of his gaze made her skin prickle. It was an odd sensation that didn't go away until she was in her room.

WEARING A WRAPAROUND SKIRT and a shell pink blouse over her swimsuit, Julie attended Sunday service the next day at one of the little churches along the highway. Afterward she took the bus to Sunset Beach where there were as many sightseers as surfers. One group was on the sand dunes watching, the other was bobbing in the ocean with their brightly colored surfboards.

She slipped off her sandals and walked barefoot on the sandy beach. A short distance from the sightseers, she took her towel from the beach bag and spread it over the sand, anchoring it from the tugging tradewinds with her shoes and suntan lotion. After removing her blouse and skirt, she folded them neatly and stowed them in the beach bag, then stretching her long legs on the towel, she began applying the sunscreen to her exposed skin. Luckily she tanned easily, but she knew about the deceptive tropic sun of the islands and didn't want to risk a burn.

Leaning back on her elbows, she watched the surfers. The waves seemed awesome when compared with the California surf she knew. Here, they looked as if they were ten feet high. A surfer on a red board caught her eye as she watched him catch an immense loft of water. He rode the wave, twisting and balancing. Julie held her breath when she saw the water gyrating around him, but he came skimming out, crouched on his board.

In absolute triumph, the surfer rode the wave into shore, milking the last curve out of the wave before it carried him to the beach. Breathless, ecstatic, he picked up his board and looked back at the ocean that he had succeded in conquering this time. Julie couldn't resist applauding. It had been a magnificent ride. He turned, sun-tanned and golden, and flashed that happy, triumphant smile at her.

"Great ride," Julie added words to her applause.

He trotted up the sand to where she sat and dropped on his knees beside her. "That wave gyrated around me like a dream."

"I saw it," she nodded.

He was still trying to catch his breath, panting from the exertion of the ride. A shining pair of brown eyes ran their gaze over her, admiration glinting openly.

"Do you surf?" he asked.

"I have," Julie admitted. "But that was a long time ago. These waves here are out of my league."

He set his board upright in the sand and sat down

beside her. "Where are you from?" He wiped the water from his face and pushed his darkly wet hair back with a raking comb of his fingers.

"California."

"I'm Frank Smith from Virginia." He offered her his hand.

"Julie Lancaster." The grip of his hand was firm, but he didn't attempt to hold hers too long.

"What are you doing here?"

"Like everybody else, I'm here to watch," she answered, glancing toward the other sightseers on the dune.

"No," he smiled. "I meant what are you doing here in Hawaii? Are you on vacation?"

"I'm working. How about you?" she returned his question.

"I'm working, too, at night as a waiter at a restaurant up the road. I came over here two years ago on vacation to see if the surf was as great as everybody said it was. I'm still here."

"I've only been here a week myself, but I already like it," Julie said to explain the paleness of her skin compared to the deep tan of his.

"Your back is beginning to look a bit red. Would you like me to put some lotion on it?" Frank Smith offered.

Julie hesitated, then agreed, "Yes, I would, thank you." As he worked the lotion over her shoulders and spine, there was a caressing quality to his touch. Julie knew he was waiting for a reaction from her, but she waited until she felt that the bare part of her back had been coated with lotion.

"That's good enough."

He didn't argue. "A bunch of us are getting together for a party tonight. Would you like to come?"

"No, I have to work tomorrow," she refused. "Maybe another time."

"Remember you said that," he smiled. For a quarter of an hour longer, he sat and talked to her. His gaze kept wavering between her and the waves swelling in the sea. Rising, he lifted his surfboard. "I guess I'll go back out. Sure you don't want to come along?"

"No, thanks." She wished him, "Catch a good one!"

With a last wave to her he waded into the water and lay on his board to paddle out where the other surfers were bobbing. Julie stayed for another hour, enjoying the sheer beauty of the surf. Sometimes she saw Frank trying a wave, but most of the time she had his red surfboard mixed up with one belonging to another surfer. After spending another hour in the hot sun, she decided to leave.

This time she took the bus to Waimea Bay. The water was glass smooth. There weren't any of the breakers that Ruel had warned her about. After a cooling swim in the crystal clear turquoise waters, Julie wisely chose to avoid the sun and relaxed in the shade of the trees in the park.

It was almost five before she caught the bus to take her back. She enjoyed the ride, even if the bus driver acted as if he owned the road where other traffic was concerned. She was free to look at the countryside.

Horses grazed in small pastures and an odd cow or two was staked out in a vacant lot. There were stands of ironwood trees with their shaggy needles crowding the beaches and green hills rising away from the road. There were sugar cane fields and, oddly enough, cornfields. A flowering shrub of some sort seemed to be blooming in almost every house-yard the bus passed.

Julie was so intent on the scenery that she almost missed her stop. Luckily she didn't. This time, though, Ruel didn't drive up behind her shortly after she got off the bus. She had to walk all the way to the house, including up the switchback road, and the calves of her legs were aching when she finally entered the house.

THE PACE of the first week set the routine for the second week. The better part of the day was spent with Debbie and her schoolwork. Sometimes in the late afternoon, Julie would swim in the pool. On her next two free days she took the bus to the Polynesian Cultural Center at Laie where the crafts and cultures of the various Polynesian tribes were kept alive.

The third week began much the same as the first two. The tradewinds dominated the weather picture and the skies remained clear. Invariably there was a small shower or two some time during each day, often when the sun was out. Liquid sunshine, it was called by the natives. Generally it was blown by the winds from rain clouds hooked by the mountain peaks. Julie didn't mind it. To her, it was like walking under a soft spray of warm water.

On Thursday, she had taken a quick dip in the pool, showered and dried her hair. Over the last two and a half weeks her skin had taken on a golden cast and her hair had lightened a shade. She took a pale green sundress from her closet and slipped it on.

It was too early yet for dinner, but the weather was too nice to stay indoors, so Julie wandered onto the *lanai* off her bedroom. She had learned the first week that at the end of the *lanai* there were stairs leading to the ground. It was perfect for swimming. She never had to track through the house in a wet suit; she could use the outside stairs to her bedroom.

Now she descended them to wander through the expansive garden surrounding the pool. It was a favorite place of hers, a private tropical paradise lined with palm trees. A massive banyan tree dominated the grounds. To support its spreading growth, the tree sent shoots downward to ultimately form new roots and trunks. As Julie wandered among its pillars, she was glad it wasn't carnivorous.

An autograph tree carried Debbie's name on one side of its large ovate leaves. Julie touched the petal of its large white flower shaded with pink. Emily had told her that in the West Indies, the leaves of the autograph tree were marked and used as playing cards.

The feathery fernlike leaves of the gray-barked jacaranda tree waved gently in the breeze. Violet blue flowers were scattered over its limbs. A magnificent Royal poinciana tree flamed like a scarlet umbrella in the garden. It was rivaled only by the peculiar tiger's claw tree. Bare of leaves, the tips of its branches were painted crimson by its claw-shaped blossoms.

Closer to the ground were the flowering shrubs. The slender delicate blossoms of the spider lily seemed lost in its clustered spray of long, wide leaves. The yellow blossoms of the plusneria were a favorite choice for *leis*. The anthurium, which on the mainland was called the frangipani, never seemed real. Its single, circular petal of brilliant red was so shiny, it looked artificial.

As Julie strolled past a hybrid hibiscus bush that hadn't been in bloom before, she saw a flower had blossomed. The other hibiscus were scarlet or deep pink, but this one was a golden yellow. She cupped it in her hand to draw it down and sniff the fragrance. The stem snapped in her fingers. After a second's hesitation, she tucked it behind her ear.

The sun was sinking behind the Waianae range. Its lengthening rays cast scarlet pink hues on the puffy white clouds and set fire to the serrated outline of the volcanic peaks. It was a beautiful and quiet display put on by nature. Julie's slow pace brought her closer to the *lanai*. There was a half-formed thought in her mind to watch the sunset from the Queen-styled wicker chair on the cobblestones.

"Having a twilight stroll, Miss Lancaster?"

Julie glanced quickly toward the shadows of the *lanai* where Ruel's voice had come from, and saw his familiar tall shape leaning against a supporting pillar.

"Yes, it's a lovely evening," she returned.

Straightening from the post, he walked leisurely toward her and stopped. The dimming light accented the masculine angles of his features while the slanting rays of the flaming sun enriched the lustrous mahogany sheen of his hair. Dressed in a golden tan sports jacket and navy blue slacks and with his shirt unbuttoned, he looked casually elegant and totally at ease. Strangely, Julie wasn't.

His gaze centered on the flower behind her right ear. "Are you looking for a lover, Miss Lancaster?"

Her hand went guiltily to the blossom. "Is that what it means when you wear it on the right side? I accidentally picked it, and it was so pretty, I decided it was a shame to throw it away, so I stuck it in my hair."

"I have no idea if that's what it means when you wear a flower there," Ruel answered her initial question. "That was simply my first thought. Perhaps because you resemble a golden flower on a pale green stem. Or maybe because when a flower blooms it issues a beguiling fragrance to lure a bee to its center, thus achieving pollination."

All the time that he was speaking in that low, conversational tone, he never glanced at the flower in her hair. He studied her mouth. Her lips felt dry. She wanted to moisten them, but she sensed it would invite a different kind of pollination. His words had nothing to do with bees and flowers and pollination; they had been an analogy of male and female desire. Her heart seemed to trip over itself trying to find its regular beat.

"I hope no bee decides to pollinate . . . the flower in my hair." Julie tried to dismiss her sudden tension with a soft laugh and deliberate obtuseness. His mouth quirked at her response, amused in a cynical fashion.

"Ruel?" Malia called to him from the dining room door to the *lanai.* "There's a phone call for you."

"Thank you, Malia, I'll be right in," he answered, never taking his eyes from Julie. "Enjoy your stroll, Miss Lancaster."

When he had gone, Julie discovered she was trembling. How ridiculous, she scolded herself. Why should she become so disturbed by a little innocent sexual sparring with words? Surely she was more mature than that. But it was several minutes before she had control of her silly nerves. By then it was almost time for dinner.

Emily Harmon was at the table when she entered through the French doors. A place was set for Ruel, but he wasn't in the room. Julie took her regular chair. Malia entered the dining room and Emily gave her a sharp look.

"He's still on the telephone, Miss Emily."

"Go ahead and serve the soup, Malia," Emily ordered.

The housekeeper served the soup—a delectable bisque. Julie was half-finished with hers when Ruel came striding into the room. He looked not the least bit upset that he was late, or that they had begun without him.

"Your soup is getting cold," Emily informed him.

Instead of walking to his chair at the head of the table, Ruel stopped at his aunt's. "Something has come up. I won't be able to have dinner with you tonight after all."

Disappointment drooped the corners of the older woman's mouth for an instant, but it was banished quickly by what could only be described as a "stiff upper lip."

"Why?" she demanded.

"I have to go into the city." He bent and lightly kissed the woman's forehead. "Don't wait up for me, Em."

The lines at the corners of his eyes crinkled when he smiled at his aunt. Julie thought she detected an affectionate tone in his voice even as he gently mocked her.

The woman sniffed in disdain. "I haven't waited up for you in years, Ruel."

"Good night." It was an all encompassing farewell that Ruel issued as he walked from the room.

Julie thought it was best not to make any comment about his departure unless Emily mentioned it. Minutes later, the quiet of the evening was broken by the roar of the sports car as it accelerated from the house.

"Why does he have to drive so fast?" Emily muttered, masking her concern with anger. She caught Julie's glance and added, "I wouldn't have been surprised if Ruel had been in an accident instead of Deborah."

Julie waited until Malia had taken away the soup dishes, then tried to introduce a different topic.

"Deborah mentioned that the cast on her left arm is to be removed next week."

The conversation became focused on Emily's niece—her schoolwork and health in general. By the end of the meal, Emily seemed more relaxed. Julie had felt the tension that had existed at the start of dinner.

The strange part was that the tension had seemed to transfer itself to her. She was restless all evening. She tried to watch a documentary on television, but it didn't hold her interest. She knew it would be hopeless trying to concentrate on a book as Emily was doing. She wandered into Debbie's room, but she was on the telephone talking to her boyfriend.

Finally Julie went to her own room. She wrote a letter to her parents and answered the one from Mrs. Kelly, who loved the *muu-muu.* For a long time she sat in one of the wicker chairs on her balcony. At half past eleven she got ready for bed even though she wasn't sleepy.

When she switched off the light and climbed into bed, the luminous dial of the radio clock kept her company. Unwillingly she watched the hours tick away. It was after two o'clock when she heard the sports car quietly drive up. She rolled onto her side and promptly fell asleep.

CHAPTER FIVE

TIME HAD GONE BY so swiftly. It seemed impossible to Julie that she had been in Hawaii for more than a month. Still, it was another weekend again—Saturday. She leaned against the balcony railing, enjoying her view of the garden. It was a riot of color—hibiscus, bougainvillea, oleanders, poinciana.

The sun was well up in the morning sky and the air was warm. Her plans for the day were only half formed—a swim in the pool, for which she was already wearing her orange bikini and beach jacket, breakfast, and a trip to the Kuhuku Sugar Mill. Julie lifted her gaze to the hills where thick stands of pine trees would randomly give way to open meadows.

As her gaze ran over the climbing hills, it was stopped by the ominous billowing of smoke. She stared for a long, heart-stopping minute. It seemed to be coming from just over the next rise. Julie raced into her bedroom, out the door and down the stairs. As she rounded the corner into the living room where the telephone was, she collided with a rock-solid object. She would have careened off it like a billiard ball, but her upper arms were clamped in a pair of steel vices.

"Where are you going in such a hurry?" Ruel demanded.

The collision had knocked the breath out of her.

It was a couple of seconds before she could manage to say, "Fire! There's a . . . fire!"

She became conscious of the well-muscled body inches from hers, aggressively male and sexually disturbing. He smelled clean and fresh with an individual scent that was faintly musky. His mouth was firm, chiseled into his features, presently curved at the corners.

The amused look was wiped from his mouth as his gaze narrowed. "Where?" His fingers dug into her soft flesh, tightening their grip.

"Just over the next hill." Julie gulped in a breath. "I saw the smoke from the balcony."

He hesitated, as if not believing her. "Show me."

"There isn't time," she protested. "We've got to call the fire department."

"You show me where it is first," Ruel insisted.

He kept a firm hold of one of her arms as he propelled her toward the doors of the lower *lanai.* Julie resisted briefly, looking frantically at the telephone just out of reach, before submitting to his order for the sake of speed. Outside the smoke was plainly visible beyond the fronds of the palm trees.

"Do you see it?" she pointed.

"Yes it's coming from our cane field," Ruel identified the fire's location.

Julie turned back toward the house. "We'd better call the fire department right away," she said decisively.

Instead of letting her go, Ruel continued his restraint of her arm, and her exasperated look caught the amused slant of his mouth.

"I said it was the cane field," he repeated.

"I know what you said," she began.

"It's being deliberately burned off." He went further in his explanation. "The fire was set on purpose. The men are keeping an eye on it. There's no need to phone the fire department."

"Oh." Julie stopped trying to pull free of his grip. "I didn't know."

"Obviously you've never seen a cane field burned." He released her arm. "It's something every island visitor should see." He gave her a considering look. "Can you ride a horse?"

"Fairly well, yes," she nodded.

"Go and change into some jeans and I'll have a horse saddled for you. We'll ride over so you can see first hand how it's done," he said.

"It'll only take me a minute," Julie promised, certain her rush of enthusiasm was for a new experience and nothing more.

Again she raced through the house for the stairs. In record time she had changed into a tan blouse and denim jeans and a pair of flat-heeled boots. She hurried down the stairs. Her foot was on the last step as Ruel walked through the front door.

"Ready?" His gaze skimmed her for his own confirmation.

"Yes." She was slightly out of breath, but it didn't interfere with the eagerness of her smile.

"The horses are all saddled and waiting outside." He held the door open for her and followed her out. "You can ride the gray. He's well trained and docile."

Ruel held the bridle while Julie mounted, and the horse stood quietly. It was an unusual experience to be looking down at Ruel when his superior height generally demanded that she look up.

"How are the stirrups? Are they short enough?"

Julie shifted a bit in the saddle checking the length. "Fine."

A blaze-faced chestnut snorted softly at Ruel when he looped the reins around its neck. It stood as quietly as her horse had when he mounted. Reining his horse around, Ruel started toward the trees and Julie followed.

She discovered a barely discernible trail wound through the trees. On the other side was a stable with two more horses in the corral. They came whinnying to the fence as they rode by. Once they were out of the trees, onto rolling but relatively flat terrain, Ruel urged his horse into a canter.

The smoke was clearly visible now. Julie expected the field to appear any minute over the next rise as Ruel angled toward it. But it was farther away than it looked. Julie didn't mind. It was an exhilarating ride. Her gray horse had a comfortable gait and kept up easily with Ruel's.

Finally they topped a hill and she saw the burning cane field below. Ruel reined in his horse and stopped it on a small knoll overlooking the field, and Julie halted her mount beside his.

"This is close enough for the horses," he said. "If we get any nearer to the fire, it might spook them."

Julie nodded her understanding. She noticed the way the gray's ears were pricked toward the crackling sounds of the flames. Its head was held alertly high. The tradewind was blowing the smoke away from them.

Half of a green field of sugar cane was blackened by the fire. Where the flames ate into the new territory, it glowed orange red. Julie frowned at the sight. Towering stalks of cane with their mauve tassels were being destroyed by the fire.

"What's wrong with the field that you have to burn it?" she asked.

"We burn our fields before we harvest the cane," Ruel explained.

"I know this is probably a dumb question," Julie said ruefully, "but why?"

"There are several reasons. The fire destroys the debris and excess plant life. At the same time, it seals sugar juice in the stalk. Plus it gets rid of all the insects and vermin that have been living in the field."

"You mean rats and snakes and such?" Julie was glad she was watching from the knoll and wasn't down where the creatures came scurrying out.

"Not snakes. We don't have any snakes in Hawaii," Ruel corrected.

"Do you mean this is an Eden without serpents?" she quipped.

"Not the reptile kind anyway," Ruel conceded, the edges of his mouth deepening in amusement. "We do have scorpions, though. They're usually very abundant in the cane fields as well as rats."

"I don't suppose there's much you can do about either of them." Her gaze was drawn to his face, liking the look of it now that his mood was not so withdrawn and cynical.

"A plantation owner some time back tried to do something about eradicating the rats. He imported the mongoose from India, but it was a dismal failure. The mongoose sleeps at night, which is when the rats are out. Now the island has another pest—the mongoose." That suggestion of a smile remained on his mouth as his gaze locked onto hers in quiet contemplation.

The gray stamped a restless foot. Julie smoothed a hand over its neck and glanced toward the burning field. "How long does it take to grow sugar?"

"From eighteen to twenty-four months, depending on the amount of moisture. It takes two thousand pounds of water to make one pound of sugar. Tourists are usually fascinated by such statistics," he observed dryly.

"Is it true?"

"Yes, it's true," he said. Resting an arm on the saddle horn, he looked at her with those cool, cynically mocking blue eyes. "So you think this is the perfect garden of Eden, with our shadowless days and absence of serpents?"

"Shadowless days?" Julie frowned at this term.

"Yes. The Hawaiian chain of islands is officially located in the tropics, the Tropic of Cancer. Since we're so near to the Equator, there are days in the summer when the sun is so directly overhead that an object—building, tree, or person—is incapable of casting a shadow."

"How fascinating!" she marveled.

Ruel glanced at his watch. "We'd better start back or you'll miss your breakfast."

Julie started to say that she didn't care, but she realized that he probably had more important things to do than show her around, so she turned her horse around and pointed it back toward the house.

HER TOUR of the Kahuku Sugar Mill that afternoon enforced what Ruel had told her and elaborated on it. Also she learned how the sugar cane was processed when she toured the restored mill and saw its colorfully painted giant flywheels turning and grinding. The tour was fascinating and informative, but not equal to the horseback ride to the burning cane field.

After church on Sunday, Julie went to the Waimea Park. It was a lush, green valley with a rippling stream and exotic plant growth. There were several historic sites being excavated—ancient moss-covered rock formations offering clues of the past. The singing water of the falls itself was worth the trip, with its natural swimming pool at the base.

It was a short walk from the falls entrance to Waimea Bay beach park. Julie had crossed the road and was walking in that direction when a van went by.

She heard somebody shout, "California! Hey, California!"

There was a squeal of brakes and she turned to see what was going on. The van had stopped on the shoulder and Frank Smith, the surfer she had met at Sunset Beach, was climbing out. Someone handed him his red board before the van took off. With his surfboard under his arm, he dashed across the highway to where Julie stood.

"Hey, California, where'd you run off to the other day? I thought you were going to wait for me. I came back out and you were gone," he accused.

"I don't remember saying I was going to wait for you." Julie was positive the subject hadn't even been raised.

"Maybe not, but I thought you would," he grinned at his own conceit. "You can't imagine what I've gone through. I don't know where you live or where you work."

"I'll bet you were really upset," she mocked. "You don't even remember my name."

"Julie Lancaster. Fooled you, didn't I?" His gaze bored into hers, his dark eyes fairly leaping with fire.

"I thought you had forgotten." Julie found his intensity a little unnerving. She started to walk again. "Nobody has ever called me California before."

"That's what you look like to me. All sunny and golden, like California." He fell in step beside her.

"That description would fit Hawaii, too," she countered.

"No, Hawaii is dark hair and dark eyes," Frank assured her.

"I see." She couldn't help smiling.

"Where are you going?" he asked.

"I thought I'd go for a swim in the bay and spend a couple of hours in the sun." Her answer was candid. With that surfboard under his arm, she doubted if Frank would settle for such a tame afternoon.

"Any objections if I come with you?"

"It's a free beach." The shrug of her shoulders said she couldn't stop him.

"Hey, California," he frowned, "are you playing hard to get or don't you really care whether I come along? What I really mean is, do you like me or not?"

His demand put her on the spot. She didn't really know what she felt. "I guess I like what I know about you, but——"

"If I was just interested in making time with you, I wouldn't remember your name after three weeks," he stated.

"No, I guess not. I'm sorry, Frank," she apologized.

"See? You even remember mine. That's a good sign."

"I suppose so," Julie laughed without really knowing why. It didn't make any sense, but then it didn't have to. It was a beautiful day and it seemed right to share it with someone.

When they reached the long, wide stretch of white coral sand Frank covered her beach bag with his surfboard before they both waded into the water. They swam and floated and played around for more than an hour before Julie finally pleaded exhaustion.

"Do you know what I miss?" he said, sinking to his knees on a corner of her beach towel. "The seagulls," he said, answering his own question.

"Seagulls." Julie suddenly realized she hadn't seen any. "Why aren't there seagulls?

"Something to do with the fact that there's hardly any difference between high and low tide here, I think. So it doesn't give them any place to find food."

"No, I guess it wouldn't," she agreed.

"I'd ask you to come out with me tonight, but I have to work," Frank said suddenly.

"I have to work tomorrow," she responded.

"What do you do?"

"I'm a teacher." She swept the wet length of her hair behind her neck letting the water trickle down her back.

"No kidding! Which school? Maybe we can have lunch together at noon," he suggested.

"I'm not teaching at a school. I'm privately tutoring a young girl who was injured in a car crash and won't be able to go back to school for a while. She doesn't want to fall back a grade in the meantime," Julie explained.

"Sounds like you've got it made."

"It's a good job," she agreed. "I work five days and have Saturday and Sunday off."

"Where do you live?" Frank noticed her hesitation. "Hey, California, I'm not going to let you get away from me without knowing where to find you again."

"It isn't a secret," Julie tried to correct that impression. "Miss Emily Harmon hired me to tutor her niece Debbie Chandler. I live there."

"Chandler," Frank repeated. "The same Chandler that has that sugar plantation about a mile or so back off the highway?"

"Yes, that's the one."

He whistled silently. "After moving in that circle for a while, I imagine it's quite a comedown to be seen with a beachbum like me."

"Don't be silly. They're very nice people. Besides, I only work for them." Julie found herself becoming defensive, but in the last month she had begun to feel very close to Debbie and her aunt. She avoided thinking about Ruel; he was an unknown quantity.

"It was just envy creeping out." Frank shrugged away his previous comment. "Well, your job rules out noon lunch dates. So how about next Friday night? There's always a party going on somewhere. And I don't have to work."

"All right," Julie agreed after only a momentary hesitation. "Friday night. What time?"

"Eight o'clock? Is that too early or too late?"

"It's fine."

"Wait until the fellows find out I have a date with my California girl," he grinned at her. "They're beginning to think I made you up out of my head—but you're real." He cupped her chin in his hand as if to reassure himself, then leaned over and kissed her.

It was a warm, exploring, first kiss, typical of many Julie had known, and she returned it in the same unaffected fashion. When Frank started to deepen the kiss, introducing passion, Julie placed a checking hand against the muscled hardness of his tanned shoulder.

His mouth lifted an inch from hers, his breath

warm against the faint dampness of the sea water cooling her cheek. "You're beautiful, California," he murmured.

"Don't rush it, Frank." She liked the casualness of their present relationship. She didn't want to plunge into something more serious until she tested the water.

Reluctantly Frank resumed his former position on the towel. The expression on his boyish handsome features said he was prepared to wait and not rush it as she had requested. With relative ease, he began talking about himself—telling Julie of the places he'd been and the things he'd done. He'd spent some time in Boston, and they began exchanging personal observations about the city.

By the time the afternoon drew to a close, Julie had enjoyed every minute of Frank's company, and it was with a degree of reluctance that she began gathering her things to catch the bus home.

Just as she was ready to go, Frank said, "Watch my board, California. There's one of my buddies down the beach. I'm going to see if I can't borrow his wheels."

Before she could respond, he was trotting off across the sun-bleached sand. The gusting tradewinds carried the name he called away from Julie's hearing. Thirty yards away, a pudgy young man turned and waited for Frank to reach him. After a brief conversation, Frank came trotting back, his tanned feet kicking up small sprays of sand. A set of keys jingled from the key ring in his hand.

"I've got it. It's parked in the lot," he told her, and

hoisted his surfboard under his arm. Grinning, he added, "We *haoles* stick together."

"*Haoles?*"

"Caucasians," he explained, and slipped a hand under her arm. "There are so many good-looking Hawaiians—you know the kind, dark and handsome—that when one of us gets a girl, we close ranks."

For some reason, Julie thought of Ruel Chandler, despite the fact that his hair was a burnt shade of brown and his eyes were blue, neither were the gleaming black of the true Hawaiian race. So she simply smiled at Frank's comment and said nothing.

The borrowed car was an aging dune buggy. Its yellow sides were splashed with red mud. The yellow stripes on its canopied top had been bleached to a cream color by the tropical sun. After stowing his surfboard in the back, Frank hopped into the driver's seat. He glanced at Julie to be sure she was safely in and started the motor. It rumbled quickly into a deafening roar. Julie suspected there was a hole in the muffler, or else no muffler at all.

"It's no Mercedes!" Frank shouted above the din, and shifted it into gear.

"Who cares." Julie retorted at an equal volume.

The dune buggy rattled and roared onto the highway. Since the vehicle possessed only a front windshield, the tradewinds whipped through the open sides, churning Julie's long hair like an eggbeater. She pushed the whirling strands away from her eyes and leaned back to enjoy the wild sense of freedom.

There was a moment of misgivings when the dune

buggy roared up the circular drive. Julie could well imagine Emily Harmon's reaction when she heard the noise outside. After her veiled warning about young men, this vehicle wasn't going to make a good first impression for Frank. In spite of that, Julie smiled.

"Here you are, all in one piece," Frank declared above the loud idling of the dune buggy.

"Surprise, surprise," she laughed.

His expression turned serious. "Don't forget, Friday night at eight sharp."

"Eight o'clock," Julie agreed.

His hand cupped the back of her neck and drew her toward him. His mouth settled onto hers—warmed by the sun and tasting of the sea. It was a hard kiss, faintly possessive but altogether pleasant. When it ended, there was a slight lift to the corners of her mouth in pleasured satisfaction. But she didn't linger for a repeat.

Stepping out of the vehicle, she offered in goodbye, "I'll see you Friday."

As the dune buggy rumbled and clattered away, she ascended the short flight of steps to the front door. Turning, she waved to Frank. In answer, he pushed the horn. A-oogah! A-oogah! The strident sound made Julie wince, then laugh. That would really impress Emily Harmon!

Upon entering the house, Julie was almost immediately met by her employer. The older woman's mouth was drawn in a disapproving line, although she tried to conceal it. Meanwhile Julie was trying to hide the amusement glittering in her light brown eyes.

"Someone gave you a ride home." Emily's observation was more in the order of a question.

"Yes, a man named Frank Smith. I met him a couple of weeks ago," Julie explained so the other woman wouldn't think she had been hasty in accepting his attention.

"At the beach?"

"Yes, he was surfing," she admitted. "He works nights," she added to assure her he wasn't a layabout. "He has this Friday night free and has asked me out."

"Did you accept?" Emily was still hesitant.

"Yes, I liked him. He seems nice and intelligent." Although it sounded like it, Julie wasn't really defending her decision. "I think I'll go and shower away this salt water."

As she glanced toward the stairs, she saw Ruel on the lower landing, and something told her he had been listening to the entire conversation. Until that moment, Julie hadn't objected to Emily's interrogation. Looking into his strongly cast features, she felt a rush of antagonism. His intelligent blue eyes regarded her with an aloof kind of amusement that was somehow challenging and insolent. After the ride in the dune buggy, she knew she looked tousled and windblown. But did she looked kissed? Ruel's expression said so.

"I do hope you're right about him," Emily remarked, "for your own sake."

"I am." Julie's response was impatient and short.

She crossed the entryway to the stairs, trying desperately to ignore the man who had started down. Her carriage lacked its usual free and easy grace. She was too conscious of the tension fluttering over her nerve ends. Forced to acknowledge his presence, she met his gaze but it was indifferent, and that fact seemed to irritate her all the more.

Tight-lipped, she passed him and hurried up the stairs. It was no use telling herself that her reaction was absurd. It was there and she couldn't change it. She swept into her room and dropped her beach bag on the floor, mindless of the granules of sand it scattered.

She marched straight into the bathroom and stripped off the tent dress belted at the waist and the bikini she wore underneath. Without taking the time to adjust the water temperature, she stepped into the shower and was blasted with cold water. Gradually it warmed to a bearable degree and she stayed beneath the hammering jets of water until she felt her muscles relax.

CHAPTER SIX

"DID YOU HAVE ANY DIFFICULTY with the third quantitative problem?" When her question went unanswered, Julie glanced up from her papers to see the young girl staring vacantly into space. "Debbie?"

Debbie seemed to come back to the present with difficulty. "What did you say? I'm sorry I wasn't listening."

Julie observed a suggestion of strain in the usually optimistic face of her teenage pupil. The last couple of days Debbie seemed to have difficulty concentrating on the schoolwork. Julie wondered if she hadn't been overdoing it and tiring the girl.

"It doesn't matter." She shrugged away her initial question and smiled. "It's Friday, so why don't we end our classes an hour early?"

"Okay." It was an enthusiastic response.

Nibbling at the edge of her lower lip, Julie hesitated, then probed, "Is something bothering you, Debbie?"

"No, nothing." The reply was too quick to be the truth. As if sensing that, Debbie plucked at the ribbon of her bed jacket. A misty film of tears darkened her eyes and there was the faintest quivering of her chin. "I'm just so tired of being in this bed." Her voice was low and tight in an effort to keep out any tremor.

In the past, Debbie had made an occasional joking remark about her confinement, but never once had she felt sorry for herself. Compassion surged through Julie at the girl's plight.

"It won't be for much longer," she offered inadequately.

"I know." Furtively, Debbie wiped at a tear that had trickled from the corner of her eye, as if ashamed of it. "I'm lucky in a lot of ways. I mean, I'm going to be all right. Thanks to you, I'm not going to fall behind in school. And my friends come to see me as often as they can. It's just that——"

Julie thought she understood. "It's just that it's Friday night, right?"

Debbie managed a tremulous smile and nodded, "Yes. All my friends have a date tonight. Ruel has a date tonight. Even you do, Julie."

Something hardened inside Julie. For some reason, she didn't want to know how Ruel Chandler intended to spend his evening. She tried not to let it show.

"That's the ultimate defection, isn't it?" she teased. "Me having a date, too."

"Gosh, no! Why shouldn't you go out with a guy? I didn't mean to make you feel guilty," Debbie insisted, her face reddening with chagrin.

"I know you didn't, Debbie." Julie smiled her understanding. "I wish I could be your fairy godmother and wave my magic wand and whisk you off to a ball tonight."

"That would be something, wouldn't it?" Debbie managed a laugh.

Setting the schoolwork aside, Julie continued in her effort to cheer the girl up. She had worked so closely with Debbie in the last month and a half that it was impossible not to be emotionally involved. Over the last two weeks or so, she had realized that she had begun to regard Debbie more as a younger sister than a student. She wasn't certain that was a good thing, but it was too late to do anything about it now.

When Emily looked in on her niece at half-past four the depressed mood had vanished and Debbie was again her optimistic, smiling self. Julie left the two of them to chat, as they usually did at the end of school time, and went to her room.

Promptly at eight, Julie decided what to wear. Since informality seemed to be the keynote in Hawaii, she had chosen a pair of white denims and a v-necked long-sleeved pullover in midnight blue velour.

Frank arrived precisely on time. Instead of the dune buggy, this time he was driving a van—a fact of which Emily Harmon took due note and on which expressed her opinion about such modes of transportation.

"I've heard that they usually have beds in the back of those vans," she informed Julie. "They're little more than motel rooms on wheels."

"That isn't altogether true." It was an effort to keep from smiling at Emily's motherly concern. "Besides, I think I can take care of myself. You'll feel better after you meet Frank," Julie assured her as he knocked at the front door.

Emily looked skeptical, but some of it melted when Julie introduced her to Frank. He was polite and courteous, but subtly charming. As Julie had found, it was difficult not to like him.

Once outside, he ran an admiring eye over her and voiced his approval of her outfit. "You look terrific, California!"

Her choice was appropriate since he was taking her to a beach party one of his friends was having. Practically everyone was there when they arrived. A bonfire was blazing on the otherwise deserted beach. Overhead the sky was studded with stars while a full moon glistened on the ocean waves. The tradewinds rustled through the needles of a stand of ironwood trees and sent the palm trees swaying. Music came from a transistor radio perched on a piece of driftwood.

After some initial ribbing of Frank about his "California" girl, they were drawn into the circle seated on the sand around the fire. One couple was popping popcorn over the open flames. A bag of marshmallows and sticks were making the circuit around the fire, with each person helping themselves and roasting their own. In addition to these refreshments, there was a nice chest filled with beer.

It was a fun-loving group with a lot of laughing and talking and story telling going on. Julie had no difficulty mixing in. She found herself liking Frank's friends as much as she liked him. At first she had been apprehensive that as the evening wore on couples would begin to drift into the privacy of the night's darkness, creating an awkward situation.

The hour grew later, but no one wandered into the shady retreat of the ironwood trees behind the stretch of beach.

The mood grew more mellow. Like other couples, Julie was leaning against Frank, her shoulders resting against his chest while his arms circled her waist. Occasionally he would nuzzle her neck, or, when she'd turn to say something to him, he would steal a kiss from her. But the exchange never became heated.

A little after midnight they ran out of firewood and beer and the party began breaking up. Frank didn't suggest they go elsewhere when they left, as if sensing that Julie would have refused anyway.

In the driveway, they sat in the van and talked for a while, the separated bucket seats making closer contact difficult. Finally Julie said it was time she went inside and Frank walked her to the steps. There they stopped to say their good-nights.

"I don't remember when I've done so little and enjoyed an evening so much. It must have been the company," Frank said as she turned to face him.

"Maybe it was the beer," Julie mocked.

"I'm not drunk," he stated quietly.

"No," she agreed. He'd had a few beers, but he wasn't drunk. "I enjoyed myself tonight, too."

When his head bent toward her, she lifted hers expectantly for his kiss, her hands sliding around his trim waist. His mouth was firm and eager against her lips. Julie responded to its pressure, letting his arms engulf her in his embrace. It was a long, lingering kiss, sweet in its intensity.

Frank continued to hold her close, murmuring against her cheek, "I wish the evening was just getting started."

"Mmmm, unfortunately it's morning already," she breathed, and made an attempt to move out of his arms.

"Don't go in, Julie." His hold tightened. "Not yet."

When she lifted her head to insist, his kiss silenced the words on her lips. At first, Julie submitted to his demands, not resisting when he pushed the silken length of her hair away from her neck and explored its curve. Instead of satisfying his ardor, she was fueling it. As his hands attempted to mould her more fully to his length, she strained to obtain a breathing space.

"Frank, please, I have to go in now." Her protest was gentle but firm.

"Not yet, honey," he insisted, and attempted to sweep her resistance aside with another passionate kiss, but this time Julie turned her face away.

Wedging her arms against his chest, she gained a little room between them. Frank continued in his attempt to change her mind. Denied her lips, he satisfied himself with the hollow below her ear. Julie didn't feel threatened by his persistence. She had warded off more serious advances in the past and felt perfectly capable of doing so again.

"That's enough, Frank." As she arched away from him, drawing her head back so he could see by her expression that she meant it, a car entered the circular drive, bathing the couple in the glare of its headlights and momentarily blinding Julie.

She recognized the sleek black sports car Ruel Chandler drove. It growled softly up the drive, looking like a prowling jungle creature with its shining eyes. By the time it had stopped behind the van, Frank had let her go. He shifted guiltily as if they had been caught doing something they shouldn't, and Julie could tell that he was suddenly very anxious to be gone. She felt a rush of impatience toward him.

"It's getting late. I'd better go," he said as he heard the car door open. He kept his voice low as if he didn't want to risk being overheard. "I'll call you, okay?"

"Sure," she agreed tightly, but Frank was already moving toward the van. Julie doubted if he had even heard her answer.

Ruel was approaching the steps where she stood. As guiltily as Frank had behaved, Julie was determined to stand her ground. She schooled her expression to be passive. After the briefest inspection of her face, Ruel paused beside her and turned to watch the van driving away.

"It seems I arrived just in time," he observed negligently.

He stood so tall beside her and so reserved that Julie felt a shiver of intimidation. Drawing herself up to her full height, she confronted him.

"I don't know what you mean by that," she retorted.

There was a hint of steel in his gaze. "Don't you?

You seemed to be in some difficulty when I drove up."

"You were mistaken, Mr. Chandler," she returned coldly. "It was nothing I couldn't handle. Nothing I haven't handled before."

"Perhaps you'll be more selective in your choice of dates in the future. Beachboys are rarely satisfied with just kisses."

The arrogance of his attitude ignited her temper. "What about you? Are you satisfied with just kisses?" she challenged. "You had a date tonight. Tell me, were you content with kisses she gave willingly, or did you seduce her?"

His eyes narrowed to cold blue slits. "I wasn't discussing my personal affairs, Miss Lancaster."

"You're a hypocrite!" Julie declared. "You're condemning Frank for behaving the way any normal, red-blooded male would, and warning me to stay away from him, but I can bet your behavior has hardly been exemplary."

"It's amazing." His mouth quirked, but with a kind of dangerous amusement. "I express concern for the reputation and well-being of a young woman who is staying in my house, and in return I'm insulted."

"You're neither interested nor concerned about what happened to me," Julie flared. "The fact that I'm living under the same roof as you are is purely incidental. You're only grabbing at it to defend yourself."

"I think I'm finally beginning to understand what you're really saying." Ruel eyed her complacently.

"Are you? I doubt it!" she snapped.

"Your ego is bruised."

His response so astounded her that Julie could only laugh out a startled, "What?"

"You're a very attractive woman, and you've probably been waiting for me to make a pass at you. Because I haven't, because I've chosen to respect you as a guest in my home, you're angry and hurt," he explained in a disgustingly reasoning tone.

For a moment Julie was so incensed she could hardly speak. She was trembling with the force of her anger. Her long fingers curled into the palms of her hands, turning them into fists clenched rigidly at her sides.

"How typically chauvinistic!" she sputtered at last. "Because I question you about what you expect from the woman you date, *you* think it's because I want to be one of them. If it weren't so pathetic, it would be funny!"

Spinning on her heel, Julie started up the steps, not trusting herself a minute longer in his company. The urge was too great to slap at that arrogantly male face. Before her foot touched the third step, an iron hand clamped itself on her arm and forced her around. On the steps, she was eye level with him, and there was something ruthless written in his tanned face that started palpitations in her chest.

"Pathetic and funny?" Ruel taunted Julie with her words. When she attempted to pull out of his grip, he simply seized her other arm and held both captive. "Do you think I haven't noticed the way you've been watching me? Do you think I haven't recognized that look in your eye? I've seen that same look of curiosity before in other women. Whether you're willing to admit it or not, you've wondered what it would be like if I kissed you."

"That isn't true!" Julie denied, and fought back a niggling doubt.

Her gaze was drawn to the savagely thin line of his mouth. She remembered that time in the garden when he had talked about flowers and bees and pollination. She experienced that same shooting sensation of danger, also that same heady excitement. He would be a hard, demanding lover, and altogether satisfying.

"Isn't it true?" The glitter in his blue eyes mocked her, as if he were capable of reading her thoughts. "You aren't the least bit interested in being kissed by me?"

"No." But it came out breathless, with little conviction behind it.

She could almost hear his silent laugh. His fingers tightened on her arm, giving her only a second's warning of his intention. Her hands came up to spread across his chest, but were trapped there as Ruel gathered her inside the steel band of his arms.

To struggle would be humiliating and useless. Julie made no further attempt to fight him, nor elude the mouth aggressively seeking out the softness of her lips. Warm and moist, it opened over hers to devour its fullness. The kiss was totally possessing, erasing from her memory the ardency of Frank's kisses that had preceded this one by only minutes.

Frank's kisses had evoked a desire to respond, but

the fierce sensuality of Ruel's kiss evoked only desire. The hard vitality of his muscular embrace seemed to burn through her, melting her into pliancy. Passion became a living thing that flamed between them. Her fingers inched up his shirt, working her arms free of their entrapment to circle his neck. She felt the satisfying crush of her breasts against the hard wall of his chest. She tried to arch closer still and lost her balance on the step.

There was little distance to fall. Encircled by his arms as she was, there wasn't any risk of falling. But the few inches she moved was sufficient to break off the kiss. When she opened her dazed eyes, her feet were on the same level with his and her head tilted back. His chiseled male face was above hers. Satisfaction at being proved right glittered in his eyes as well as the fire of desire.

When his head bent toward hers, Julie rose on tiptoe to meet him halfway. It seemed impossible, but the second kiss was more electrifying than the one before. Now that there was no more need to force her into compliance, his hands spread over her lower spine to fit her curves more fully against his male contours, and Julie gloried in the differences between them.

Her lips parted under the probing demand of his. The caress of his hands was creating an urgency within her that she had never experienced before. She clung to him, her fingers sliding into his thick hair, pressing his mouth more firmly against her own, finding ecstasy in the pain of wanting.

An uncontrollable shudder of need hammered

through her when his hand slipped under her sweater and encountered her bare flesh. It was fire against fire—their body heat consuming each other. His hand sought and found her breast, cupping it in his palm. Her heart ran away with itself, beating so fast that its number couldn't be counted. She no longer had dominion over her heart or her soul.

"Ruel? Ruel, is that you?" Emily Harmon's imperious voice broke the stillness of the night. It came from somewhere above them and ripped their kiss apart. "Ruel?"

His hand pressed Julie's face against his shirt as if to silence any outcry from her. "Yes, Em, it's me," he answered.

The part of her mind that could think marveled at his control. She doubted if she had the strength to speak. She was aware of the way her body was trembling against his—not from fear, but she wondered if he thought so.

"I thought I heard you drive in a while ago. What are you doing out there?" his aunt demanded.

With her senses behaving more rationally, Julie was able to tell that Emily Harmon was speaking from a second floor window. The shadows of the front *lanai* concealed the two of them from her view.

"Having a cigarette," Ruel answered. "It's late, Em. You should be in bed. You need your rest."

"So do you," was the snappish reply, followed almost immediately by a sigh, "Julie hasn't come home yet. I'm worried about her. We don't know anything about that young man she went out with. He——"

"Julie is here," he interrupted.

"Julie is here?" There was disbelief in the woman's voice.

"Yes, she came back the same time I did," Ruel said truthfully, and slowly loosened his hold of her. "She's here on the steps with me."

"Julie?"

"Yes, M . . . " Her first attempt to answer was so weak that she had to clear her throat and try again. "Yes, Miss Emily."

"You're home!" the woman declared now that she had the evidence with her own ears.

"Yes, I got back a little while ago." Julie stole a glance at Ruel, who was now standing a full step away from her. He was lighting a cigarette, and in the flame, his face betrayed no emotion. The torrid embrace did not seem to have shattered him the way it had her.

"Good." Emily Harmon sounded uncertain, as if she felt there was something more she should say, but she didn't know what. "I'll turn in now. Don't you two stay out there too long. It's late."

"We'll . . . we'll be in directly," Julie promised.

Her words were followed by a silence—a tense silence. Ruel shook a cigarette partially out of its pack and offered it to her, but she shook her head in wordless refusal and he replaced the pack in his shirt pocket.

"I owe you an apology, Julie," he said in a controlled, even voice. "With so many of Debbie's girl friends constantly going in and out of the house, I've always made it a rule never to become involved with them, regardless of the provocation."

There was a constriction in her throat. "I'm not one of Debbie's girl friends," she said tightly.

"I never become involved with any woman who works for me, directly or indirectly. I have no excuses for my action." He didn't sound remorseful. "You were so self-righteous that I kissed you the first time just to prove you were wrong. That alone was stupid and arrogant on my part."

"And the second time?" Julie didn't know why she was asking.

"The second time was because you were so damned passionate the first." His anger was tinged with amusement—at her.

Julie wished she could deny it, but she was fully aware of her abandoned response. There was a proud lift to her chin as she turned to meet his gaze. His was aloof yet watchful, studying her reaction.

"I have no excuse, either," she said. "I'm not going to try to blackmail you with this, if that's what you're thinking. I'm no more interested in having an affair with you than you are with me. This was a regrettable incident, one that I'm all in favor of forgetting."

"My sentiment exactly," Ruel agreed.

"If that's settled, then, I think I'll go in," she said stiffly.

He shrugged and looked away. "There isn't anything more to keep you out here."

"No, there isn't." And she felt sick inside.

Her legs were trembling as she walked to the front door. Any second, she expected him to say . . . . What did she want him to say? That he loved her? No. There was undeniably a powerful physical attraction between them, but sheer chemistry was not love.

Closing the door, she leaned weakly against it. She fully understood his reason for not wanting to let this mutual desire they had experienced become anything more. Sooner or later it would become awkward for both of them. It was sensible and logical to end it now.

"Julie? Julie?"

Someone was whispering her name. For a heart-stopping minute, she thought it might be Ruel, but the voice had been female and young. It was Debbie. For a second, Julie toyed with the idea of ignoring it, but that was too cowardly. Glancing briefly toward the stairs, she moved silently across the entryway to the girl's bedroom.

"How was your date?" Debbie whispered when she appeared in the doorway.

"It was fine," Julie answered, and immediately changed the subject. "Why aren't you asleep?"

"I don't know. Insomnia, I guess." The indifference in her voice said Debbie was concerned. "Ruel came home the same time you did, didn't he?"

"Yes." Julie was relieved that there was no light on.

"He's outside, smoking a cigarette."

"I thought I heard the two of you arguing."

"Arguing?" Julie repeated, to stall for time. "You must have been mistaken."

The answer seemed to satisfy Debbie. "Where did you go on your date?"

"To a beach party." That seemed such a long time ago. So much had happened since then.

"That must have been fun—and romantic," Debbie added suggestively.

"It was. And it was also tiring. You may not be sleepy, but I am. I'll tell you all about it in the morning," Julie suggested.

"Are you going to see him tomorrow?"

See whom? Ruel? That was Julie's first thought. Then she realized Debbie meant Frank. Tomorrow was Saturday, her day off. She suddenly wondered how she was going to fill the hours. The last thing she wanted to do was think.

"No, not tomorrow," she said. "I'll talk to you in the morning. Good night, Debbie." She slipped out of the door before Debbie could ask more questions that Julie didn't feel like answering.

Upstairs, she lay in her bed another hour before she heard Ruel walk down the hallway to his room. Sue Ling, Debbie's nurse, had the next bedroom to Julie's. It separated her room from Ruel's. As she lay in bed, aware of her body's aching needs, the distance seemed to make the situation almost untenable.

It wouldn't last, Julie assured herself. She would forget it.

CHAPTER SEVEN

A MONTH LATER, Julie was silently congratulating herself for overcoming the whole unfortunate incident so successfully. It had taken on the aspect of a dream that seemed real at the time, but had faded into a distant memory with the passage of days.

It helped that there were so few occasions when she had to be in Ruel's company. Even during those times there was always someone around, either his aunt or Debbie, to keep any mention of the incident from cropping up. Ruel treated her in the same distant fashion that he had before it happened.

If there were times when she looked at him and had the sudden, vivid memory of his hard mouth destroying her with its kiss or the feel of his tautly muscled body imprinting itself on hers, or the intimate caress of his hands finding the places that excited her, Julie never consciously admitted it.

When she walked into the dining room that evening and saw Ruel seated at the head of the table, she gave him a cool smile as was her custom and took her usual chair on his left. The beat of her heart remained steady, if a trifle loud in her ears, and there wasn't the slightest tremor in her hands as she spread the linen cloth across her lap.

"You look lovely this evening, Julie," Emily Harmon commented from across the table. "Is that caftan new?" I don't recall seeing you wear it before."

"Yes, I bought it in one of those shops at the Kuilima resort." The delicate pastel shades of yellow and pink in a Hawaiian print had caught her eye. She had purchased it during a moment of self-indulgence, knowing she should save her money.

"The color suits you. Don't you think so, Ruel?" Emily enlisted her nephew's opinion.

"It's very attractive," he agreed dutifully.

"Thank you." Julie wanted to applaud herself for replying with such composure.

"It's so good to have you with us, Julie," said Emily, the statement seeming to come out of the blue. "You've almost become one of the family since you arrived—you fit in so well."

Without realizing it, Julie darted a glance sideways at Ruel, but he appeared not to have heard what his aunt said. Immediately she curved her mouth into a smile and directed it at the older woman.

"It's remarkably easy with people like you," she returned the compliment to the giver.

"I don't know why I haven't said it before, but I feel we're truly fortunate to have you to tutor Debbie," Emily added. "You were very highly recommended to us. At the time I was worried that you wouldn't be able to obtain a leave of absence from your teaching post. You were an American history teacher at the high school level, weren't you? I'm relieved they were able to find a replacement for you at such short notice."

Somehow the conversation had never got around to what she had been doing before she came to Hawaii. They had talked of her family and her college years and of life in Boston. Julie had always presumed Emily Harmon knew she had been available for this job. Now she was at a loss as to how to correct the erroneous impression the woman had.

"You were an American history teacher?" Ruel took up the subject as if to cover Julie's silence.

"I . . . I majored in American history, yes," she hesitated. "But, after college, I wasn't able to find a job teaching, except for tutoring Carla Rifkin."

Emily's soup spoon was halfway to her mouth. It stayed there for a second before she returned it to the soup bowl. Julie was uncomfortably conscious of Ruel's gaze studying her with a shrewd alertness.

"I thought you were teaching," Emily commented.

"I was employed as a substitute teacher," Julie explained.

"You know how it is when you're fresh out of college—you may have the degree, but no experience."

"What were you doing?" Ruel asked with casual interest.

Julie directed her answer to Emily, trying not to sound defensive. "I was working as a waitress. Mrs. Grayson knew—I thought she'd told you."

Out of the corner of her eye she saw the brief quirking of Ruel's mouth and resolutely kept her gaze from straying to him. Considering his arrogant attitude toward most things, he probably regarded her previous position as somehow demeaning. The thought stiffened her neck, thrusting her chin slightly forward.

"What a deplorable waste of your education," was Emily Harmon's reaction. "With your qualifications, I should think they would have overlooked your lack of experience. I don't see why they regarded it as being so critical. Did they give you an explanation?"

"They doubted my ability to control a classroom of high school students," Julie answered frankly.

"Yes, especially the male members," Ruel inserted dryly.

"Yes, especially the male members," she admitted, her jaw tightening.

"Simply because she's young and attractive? That's unfair," protested Emily.

"It would be unfair to the class. Julie would have to divide her energies between teaching and handling the fresh boys in the group," Ruel declared. "They would spend more time ogling her shape than attending to the subject at hand."

"Oh, really?" Julie seethed. "*You* don't seem to have any difficulty repressing your desires when you're around me!"

Their eyes clashed and locked, charging the air with a volatile tension. All pretense that either of them had forgotten the incident on the *lanai* was dissolved by the heat of her accusation.

"Julie, I——" Emily Harmon's hesitant and confused voice made Julie sharply aware of what she had said and how rude it had sounded.

"I'm sorry," she apologized, breaking the electric

contact with Ruel's eyes. "But so many high school principals have made similar remarks about my looks that I've become rather sensitive about the issue. I shouldn't have lashed out like that."

"I'm sure it's been very frustrating for you," Emily agreed. "I know Ruel understands that you didn't mean it personally."

"Of course." Ruel quietly enforced his aunt's comment, but Julie wondered if she were the only one who heard the suppressed violence in his deadly calm tone. The telephone rang and he pushed his chair away from the table. "I'll answer it . . . it's probably the call I've been expecting. Excuse me."

"Don't be long," Emily admonished, but received no response from Ruel as he left the room.

From experience, Emily didn't hold up the meal for him. They were halfway through the entrée when he returned to his seat at the head of the table. Malia was there almost instantly to serve him his meal.

"*Mahimahi*," Ruel identified the broiled fish on his plate. "It looks excellent, Malia."

"It is," Emily stated, and sought confirmation from Julie. "Isn't it?"

"It's delicious," she agreed. "Is it a tropical species?"

"It's a dolphin," Ruel told her.

"A dolphin?" Her eyes rounded in startled dismay.

"Relax," he mocked. "It's the fish dolphin, not the mammal. You aren't eating Flipper."

His baiting tone irritated her. She wondered if he

were deliberately trying to rile her and pay her back for her remark. That was foolish, of course.

"Don't tease her, Ruel," his aunt reproved. "It's a common error made by many visitors to the islands."

But Julie didn't want to be defended by Emily. "*Mahimahi* is the Hawaiian name for the dolphin, then?" she asked, subtly altering the subject.

"Yes." It was Emily who responded, as Julie expected. It started a discussion of the Hawaiian language and kept the conversation away from personal topics.

BY THE END of the week, Julie found it hadn't been so easy to forget how quickly she had flared at Ruel's comment about her looks. She hadn't become as indifferent to him as she had thought; her feelings smouldered beneath the surface. It was an unsettling discovery as she had been convinced that she had pushed him from her mind and her senses.

A car whizzed by and she stepped quickly back to avoid being splashed by the water on the road. A steady drizzle was falling, but the temperature was warm. The sunshine of the morning had been replaced by overcast skies and rain.

Shielding her eyes from the heavy drizzle, Julie peered down the highway for a glimpse of the bus. When she'd left the house that morning, she hadn't prepared for any change in the weather, and in consequence she'd had no protection from the rain. Her hair was plastered to her head, a gleaming dark honey shade. She was almost soaked to the skin—

her wet clothes clinging to her. But at least it was warm!

There was more than half of the afternoon left. Since the weather showed little indication of improving, Julie had decided she might as well spend the rest of her Saturday back at the house writing letters. Unfortunately there was no sign of the bus. She debated whether or not to take shelter in the grocery store behind her, but she was afraid she wouldn't see the bus coming and would miss it.

A convoy of military trucks and jeeps went by. A few of the soldiers whistled and waved when they saw her standing at the bus stop. Sighing, Julie hunched her shoulders against the light rain. The burnt red volcanic soil at her feet was turning into mud.

The honking of a horn lifted her gaze from the ground, and the sight of a glistening black sports car slowing to a stop brought an immediate tensing of her muscles. She saw Ruel lean across and open the passenger door, his hard-bitten features looking out at her, elemental and male.

"Get in," he ordered.

Julie took a step backward. "I'm all wet."

"The water will wipe off." Impatience thinned the line of his mouth. "I'm not going to beg you to ride with me. Make up your mind, I'm holding up the traffic."

Julie glanced down the road and saw the cars lining behind him. The bus still wasn't in sight. Logic insisted that she accept his offer. After only a second's hesitation, she slid into the passenger seat and closed the door. Immediately Ruel put the car in gear and it accelerated forward.

"Thanks for stopping." Courtesy demanded that she make some acknowledgement of his action regardless of what his motivation might have been.

There was no response. Her face was beaded with rain water. She wiped at it with a wet hand and a handkerchief was offered her. She glanced at him as she accepted it. He faced the road, his bold profile masking any expression.

The windshield wipers swish-swished back and forth in a hypnotic rhythm. Julie wiped her face dry with the handkerchief. The faint, tantalizing scent of his after-shave lotion clung to the linen material, a musky fragrance that seemed indicative of his obvious manhood. That wasn't something Julie wanted to notice about him, not in the close quarters of the car.

"Are you cold? Would you like me to turn the car heater on?" Ruel asked, distantly polite.

"No, it isn't necessary. I'm just wet." She was nervous, disturbed by his nearness and unwilling to admit it.

His handkerchief was damp, as she wadded it into her hands and held it on her lap, reluctant to return it to him in its present sodden condition. The heavy silence between them was unnerving. Julie longed to end it, but was afraid she would begin chattering like a nervous schoolgirl. She felt irritated and wished she had waited for the bus regardless of the drizzle.

Directly ahead of them, a shaft of sunlight pierced the clouds and created a rainbow in the sky. She tried to concentrate on the way the colors faded into each other, instead of the man behind the wheel.

"Dammit! Will you relax?" Ruel growled savagely, and she nearly jumped out of her seat.

"I am," she lied quickly and badly.

"You are as nervy as a cat who's used up eight lives." His mockery was harsh and deliberately cutting.

Julie collected her poise. "If I seem uncomfortable, it's probably because I am," she retorted. "Who wouldn't be if they were sitting around in wet clothes?"

His gaze sliced over her, taking swift note of the way the knit material of her top damply moulded itself to the shapely roundness of her breasts. Heat coursed through her veins, warming her skin, but almost immediately his attention was back on the rain-slick highway in front of him.

"We'll be at the house soon and you'll be able to change into some dry clothes." Once again his voice and expression were smooth and emotionless.

As far as Julie was concerned, they couldn't get there soon enough. She made some meaningless comment to him and stared out of the side window. She didn't draw an easy breath until Ruel stopped the car in the circular drive in front of the house.

"Thanks for the ride." She didn't even glance at him as she said it, pushing open the door and using the excuse of the rain to bolt into the house.

In the entryway, she heard a trio of laughing voices from Debbie's room and guessed her girl friends were visiting her. She didn't see either Emily or Malia as she hurried up the stairs to her room.

Stripping out of her wet clothes, she put on a short terry cloth beach jacket. She was shaking, but she didn't know whether it was from nerves or because she was chilled from her wet clothes. The first seemed the most likely. Angry with herself, she began toweling her hair dry with a roughness that hurt.

A knock at her bedroom door brought an automatic response, "Come in."

Julie turned as it opened. Ruel walked in and her hands ceased holding the towel. It slid from the darkly golden tangle of her long hair to settle around her neck.

Why didn't he leave her alone, she thought wildly, and demanded, "What do you want?" Her voice was sharp to that of rudeness.

His gaze traveled down the length of her tanned legs before meeting the challenging directness of her eyes. She had nothing on beneath the jacket, which he obviously guessed. She was grateful it came down over her hips. He was holding a small tray with a cup and saucer and teapot on its surface.

"I asked Malia to fix you some hot tea," he answered evenly, and walked into the room to set it on the desk. "After your drenching, I thought you might like a hot drink."

"Why all this sudden show of concern for my well being?" Julie couldn't keep the sarcasm out of her voice. "I thought you were worried about becoming involved with women who worked for you," she lashed out in frustration.

In a single long stride Ruel was in front of her, roughly grabbing her arms. The tautness of anger was etched in his strong features. He hauled her against his chest, his grip lifting her onto her toes. His mouth was so near she couldn't breathe. Her bare legs rubbed against the smooth material of his slacks and the solidly muscled thighs they covered. His body heat seemed to envelop her. There was a deafening rush of blood in her ears as she waited for the punishment of his kiss.

It never came. Instead she was released as abruptly as she had been seized. While she stumbled backward, Ruel walked out of the room, slamming the door behind him. Waves of disappointment rushed through her. She was faced with the humiliating possibility that she had goaded him deliberately, expecting the retaliation of an embrace. She slumped into the desk chair and buried her face in her hands. The tea was lukewarm before she got around to drinking it.

AFTER DINNER that evening, Julie sat in the living room with Emily, painfully conscious of Ruel's presence. It was a strain to concentrate on what Emily was saying and appear interested, but she tried.

"You look pale, Julie," the woman observed. "Are you feeling all right?"

"Fine," she insisted with a tense smile. The narrowed glance of skepticism she received made her add, "I have a slight headache, that's all."

"Ruel mentioned to Malia that you were caught in the shower this afternoon. Maybe you're coming down with something," Emily suggested.

"I don't think so," Julie denied. "It's just a common headache, not the common cold."

"Perhaps some fresh air will help it," said Ruel. He stood beside the French doors that led onto the ground floor *lanai*. "It isn't raining anymore. Why not take a short stroll outside?"

"Yes, I think that's a good idea," she agreed eagerly, glad to escape the stifling atmosphere of the house.

Rising from the sofa, she crossed the room to the double doors Ruel held open for her. It wasn't until she had stepped onto the veranda that she realized he intended to accompany her, and she glanced back into the room at Emily. There was nothing in the woman's expression to indicate that she found anything wrong with the situation.

As soon as they were out of earshot, Julie said, "I want to apologize for what I said and the way I behaved today. You didn't deserve it, and I'm sorry."

"Apology accepted," he acknowledged simply and with an air of diffidence. "Although it doesn't solve our problem, does it?"

Her gaze skittered away, not quite able to meet his look sideways. "Problem? I don't know what you mean."

"Don't you?" The rejoinder was aloofly amused.

"No, I'm afraid I don't know," Julie insisted, continuing to walk straight ahead. She was glad of the darkness and its concealing shadows.

The touch of Ruel's hand on her waist halted her. Applying slight pressure, he turned her to face him. She forced herself to breathe evenly and not pay any attention to the fluttering of her pulse. As long as his touch remained impersonal, she wasn't going to make a fool of herself by resisting.

"Pretending hasn't made it go away, *Kulie*," he said.

His hands lightly spanned her waist without making any attempt to lessen the distance between them. Julie felt herself becoming putty in his hands and pivoted away from him while she still had some backbone. Ruel let her turn away, but he didn't release her.

"I don't know what you're talking about," she repeated. "What was that you called me?"

"*Kulie*. That's your name in Hawaiian," Ruel answered.

"How fascinating." There was a faint tremor in her voice as she attempted to change the subject. "What is yours?"

"It's an old family name. Ruel doesn't have an equivalent in Hawaiian." Patience seemed to dominate his answer.

"I see," she murmured.

"We're going to have to come up with another solution for our problem," Ruel reverted to his earlier discussion.

An odd weakness attacked her knees. "As far as I'm concerned, we don't have a problem, Mr.

Chandler." She took a quick step forward, moving out of his unresisting hold. Warily she stayed out of his reach. "If you'll excuse me, I have some letters to write." She started toward the outside set of stairs that led to the upper *lanai* and her bedroom. "Good night."

"Running isn't the answer, Julie." His voice carried quietly to her, but he didn't try to stop her. "You'll have to face it sooner or later."

Julie infinitely preferred later. Tonight she couldn't cope with the potency of his attraction. She certainly couldn't be as calm and reasonable about it as Ruel sounded.

The French doors to her bedroom were unlocked. She opened them and paused. Glancing over her shoulder, she saw Ruel standing near the chaise lounge by the pool. The red glow of a cigarette was in his hand. In an abrupt movement that suggested anger, he crushed out the cigarette beneath his heel. Jamming his fists into the pockets of his slacks, he turned away from the house.

Julie could only guess at the cause for his action. This physical thing between them didn't please him anymore than it pleased her. He was probably irritated with himself for even mentioning it. As for a solution. . . . She went into her bedroom and closed the doors. An affair was the obvious answer. But if it burned itself out before Debbie was better, how would she be able to stay here in the same house with him?

CHAPTER EIGHT

RUEL WAS SELDOM at the house during the week that followed. On the one evening he did spend at home, he made no attempt to speak to Julie or draw her aside. She kept telling herself she was relieved that he had decided not to pursue the matter. If she weren't totally convinced she didn't admit it.

On Saturday morning she joined Emily for breakfast at nine o'clock on the *lanai.* The sun was warming the cobblestoned floor and the air was fragrant with the scents of many tropical flowers blooming in the garden. Julie helped herself to the slices of fresh pineapple on the table and sat in a rattan chair next to Emily.

"It's a gorgeous day, isn't it?" Julie remarked.

"It couldn't be better," the woman agreed. "What are your plans for today?"

"I thought I'd go into Honolulu. I haven't been there yet, and—" she lifted her shoulders in an expressive shrug and laughed "—what would I say to my friends if they asked me whether I'd been to Waikiki or not?"

"I suppose that's true. But personally I don't think you're missing anything." Emily's opinion of the commercially developed area hadn't changed.

"Besides, there are several other places of interest I want to see in Honolulu," Julie defended her decision.

"Yes, there are a few," Emily conceded. "You're welcome to use the car."

"No, I'll take the bus. I'm not familiar with the streets. Trying to find my way in traffic is not my idea of fun anyway. And there's always the problem of finding a place to park." The disadvantages outweighed the other considerations in Julie's opinion.

"It's quite a long bus ride," the woman cautioned.

"I don't mind," she insisted. "It will give me time to look at the countryside."

"What will?" Ruel walked onto the *lanai.*

"Good morning, Ruel." Emily offered him a cheek, which he dutifully bent to kiss before helping himself to the coffee.

Dressed in a loose-fitting Hawaiian shirt of white cotton and light blue slacks, Ruel walked behind Julie to sit in a chair beside her. Setting his cup on the table, he buttered a slice of sweet bread.

"What will give you time to look at the country?" he repeated his question without glancing at her.

"Julie is taking the bus into Honolulu this morning," his aunt explained. "I was just warning her that it would be a long ride, what with all the stops it has to make along the way."

"I'm going downtown this morning. You're welcome to ride with me," he offered indifferently.

Julie hesitated, a polite refusal forming on her lips, but Emily was speaking before she had the chance to respond. "How thoughtful of you, Ruel!" she exclaimed. "It's the perfect answer."

"I wouldn't want to put you to any trouble. I

know you have business to attend to and——" Julie tried delicately to get out of accepting.

"It wouldn't be any trouble," Ruel assured her blandly, a glint of challenge in his blue eyes. "I have to drive to Honolulu anyway. I can drop you wherever you like."

"Of course he can," Emily inserted. "It would certainly be more comfortable than riding on a crowded bus. And you'll still be able to see the country."

She was left with little option but to accept his offer. "In that case, I'll ride with you," she agreed.

After breakfast, Julie went upstairs to collect her purse while Ruel brought the car around to the front. Emily waved goodbye to them from the house. It was an hour's drive into the city and she tried to think of what they could talk about for all that length of time.

"You make this drive almost every day. It must get tiresome."

"Sometimes," he agreed, "especially if the traffic is heavy. It also gives me time to think—to sort out various projects and problems. Views like that—" he indicated the one ahead of them "—keep it from becoming too monotonous."

They had just started down the switchback road that led to the highway, and their height provided a panoramic view of the coastline. The ocean was a pale blue near the shore where the reefs were and a deep, rich blue beyond—the color of lapis lazuli. White strips of beach were broken by clumps of rusty black lava rock rising from the golden sands.

The vivid green of the abundant tropical growth on the land provided a brilliant contrast. Jutting out to sea was the headland of the Waianae range of mountains.

"It is spectacular," Julie agreed. Even that seemed an understatement. Before she could take it all in, the car had made the last curve and the road was leveling out toward the highway.

At the intersection, Ruel waited for a lull in the traffic before turning onto the road. Not wanting to distract him, Julie kept silent. As they drove along the coast a few minutes later, she couldn't think of anything to say again. They passed a small beach with surfers bobbing in the waves.

"What happened to your friend?" Ruel slid her a lazy, inquiring look.

"Frank? He's around." Her answer was carefully nonspecific.

"Don't you see him anymore?"

"Yes." Which was true. She had simply avoided going out with Frank—mainly because she knew his affection was more serious than hers. She liked him, but she didn't want it to go any further than that.

"You haven't gone out with him lately," Ruel commented.

"He works nights," she said as if that was the explanation. "I usually see him sometime during the weekend—usually Sunday.

"Are you meeting him in town today?" Ruel circled the rotary to the Honolulu turnoff.

"No," Julie looked out of the window. Short

stands of grass punctuated a field of ploughed earth in a semblance of rows. "Is that sugar cane?"

"Yes, a new field. As it grows, it will spread out and bush until it's as thick as this next one." He indicated the one just ahead, towering thick and green close to the road, tassels waving over the top. "When you see tassels in a field, the cane stalks are usually sweet. This particular field is about ready to be fired."

"I enjoyed seeing that the day we rode out to your field," she said without thinking, a look of pleasure lighting her eyes.

She remembered the interlude vividly—the two of them riding across the meadow toward the smoke, pausing on the knoll to watch the red wall of fire creep through the field. There had been an easiness between them that Julie wished she could recapture. "Have you been riding lately?" Ruel asked.

"On horseback? No, I haven't." She shook her head.

"You're welcome to ride the gray whenever you like, take him down for a run on the beach sometime. Tell Malia and she'll have Al saddle him for you," he explained.

"Thank you, I might do that some weekend." Although she silently thought it might be a bit lonely riding without him. She quickly pushed that thought out of her mind.

Abruptly, it seemed, the cane field was behind them. Now, on either side of the road grew low, spiky plants. It took Julie a second to recognize them as pineapple. The fields were geometrically designed with rounded corners and straight rows.

Ruel noticed her rapt expression as she gazed out of the window. "You haven't seen pineapple growing before?"

"No," she admitted.

The car began perceptibly to slow its fast pace. Julie thought it was to give her a better view, but instead Ruel pulled onto the shoulder and stopped the car. In the row of plants paralleling the highway, she could see the conical fruit of the pineapple, growing as an offshoot of the plant.

"They're harvesting over there." Ruel pointed to a machine farther down the field straddling the rows with a conveyor belt, complete with lights for nighttime picking, stuck out from its side like a long arm. The field hands walked behind the arm, dropping the pineapple on the belt where it rode to the machine.

"You'll notice the pickers are wearing a lot of clothes—long-sleeved shirts and jackets, pants, and boots and gloves. Pineapple plants are wickedly sharp, so the pickers need a lot of protection from the spiky leaves."

Julie watched the process for several minutes before guiltily realizing that this was all very old to Ruel, who had seen it a thousand times or more before. She cast him a rueful look.

"I'm sorry. You should have said something rather than let me hold you up like this," she protested.

"It was my idea to stop in the first place." His mouth slanted into a brief smile. "If I weren't willing to be delayed, I wouldn't have done that. We'll leave when you've seen all you want."

"I have," Julie insisted.

"Besides—" Ruel paused to check the oncoming traffic; drove back onto the highway and then continued his sentence "—I couldn't let my sister's teacher be in ignorance about pineapples."

"That would be bad, wouldn't it?" she smiled.

"I gain something from it, too," he said.

"What?" She was curious.

"Looking through the field through your eyes, it becomes something new for me. I stop taking it for granted," explained Ruel.

The traffic became heavier as they passed Schofield Barracks and the town of Wahiawa. The pineapple fields were left behind and the terrain became rolling and wooded. There was a predominance of trees with canopied, umbrellalike limbs that Julie recognized as the monkeypod. From this tree came the many wooden bowls and dishes that were the standard souvenir of Hawaii. Just as suddenly, it seemed, the open country gave way to a mass of towns running together. Highway signs pointed to Pearl Harbor, Honolulu and Waikiki.

"Where would you like me to take you?" Ruel asked.

"Wherever it would be most convenient." Julie had no specific destination in mind. She had the whole day to sightsee the downtown area.

"Will the yacht harbor be all right? It isn't far from the center of Waikiki," he told her.

"That will be perfect."

Seconds later, he was stopping the car on a side street near the curb. The tall masts of sailing boats rose in the distance, crowded together in a confusing mixture. For a ride that had begun with so many misgivings on Julie's part, she was sorry to have it end.

"Thanks for bringing me," she said.

"Enjoy your day," was his parting remark with no mention of seeing her later, or possibly giving her a ride back.

She stepped onto the sidewalk and waved as Ruel drove away. She had a decidedly let down feeling as she started down the street alone. Resolutely, she told herself it was the way she wanted it.

After more than an hour of wandering through the tourist shops, she picked up some literature on places to see in Honolulu. From the luxury hotels, along the beach, she journeyed to the Punchbowl—an extinct crater that had become the cemetery of the Pacific. From there, she traveled to downtown Honolulu and walked through Chinatown, then on to the State Capitol building and Iolani Palace where the ruling Hawaiian monarchs had lived. The Palace was now a museum. A visitor at the Palace suggested to Julie that she would enjoy the Bishop Museum, where there were several exhibits regarding the Polynesian cultures and their contribution to Hawaii.

It was afternoon when Julie arrived at the Bishop Museum on the mountainside of Honolulu. With her admission paid, she went to the snack bar in the center of the courtyard before touring the exhibits.

The old, massive stone building had been a summer palace of the Hawaiian monarchy years ago. Its beauty was evident in the beautifully carved wood panels lining the stairway and the banisters and woodwork. Most impressive was the main room with its ceiling rising several floors high.

Hanging from the ceiling was the skeleton of a whale, one side exposed and the other sculpted out of papier-mâché to show the bulk of the monolith of the ocean. On each floor were exhibits of various cultures and eras. From the wrought iron railings around each floor could be seen the whale and the typical Hawaiian hut built on the main floor.

On display in the museum was a magnificent collection of feathered cloaks once worn by Hawaiian royalty. The rich yellow and red and black designs were created by taking single feathers from exotic birds and weaving them into a solid fabric. It had taken years to make one robe, but the colors had not faded with the passage of time.

Julie worked her way to the main floor. As she started down the last staircase, she happened to glance up from the steps. Waiting at the base was Ruel, a hand resting on the curved banister, a half-smile curving his mouth. Her heart skipped a beat and exploded like a rocket.

"How—How did you know I was here?" she stammered.

"I asked myself 'Where would a history teacher go if she were sightseeing?' The only logical answer was a museum. I simply had to go around until I found the right one," he answered smoothly.

"You haven't been to every museum?" Julie protested.

"Only the three obvious choices—Iolani Palace, the mission house, and here." He glanced around the main floor. "Have you seen it all?"

"Yes," she nodded, still stunned to find him waiting for her.

"Would you like a ride home?" Ruel asked, studying her with a sideways tilt to his mahogany dark head.

For the first time Julie glanced at her watch, surprised to find she had spent more than three hours at the museum. It was a few minutes before four o'clock.

"Yes, I would." It seemed an unnecessary answer to an unnecessary question.

Tucking a hand under her elbow, Ruel guided her to the exit. In the parking lot was his sports car. "What did you think of the city?" He unlocked the door and held it open for her.

"I liked it." Her answer was automatic, given before she thought about what had prompted his question. "You were wondering if Emily had colored my thinking?" she laughed as he slid behind the wheel.

"Did she?" His laughing glance admitted she was right. "Em is convinced Waikiki is one step away from Coney Island."

"Oh, I admit all the tall buildings didn't seem to fit my idea of Hawaii, but it has a lot of redeeming qualities."

"Such as?" Ruel wanted to know as he left the parking lot and fought a way into the traffic.

"The people," Julie decided. "There's such a mixture."

"Oahu, the Gathering Place. That's the island's nickname," he explained. "It certainly is true. People watching is the most popular pastime in Honolulu."

"I can believe that," she laughed softly.

"What haven't you seen since you've been here?" Ruel asked in all seriousness.

"I haven't been to Pearl Harbor yet, or the Arizona Memorial," Julie answered.

"Have you been to the Pali lookout?" Instead of making a turn toward the ocean and the highway home, Ruel turned the car toward the mountain range rising above Honolulu.

Her glance was quizzical. "Pali? Is that the goddess of volcanoes?"

"No, that's Pele. *Pali* is the Hawaiian word for cliff. The Pali is the gap through the Koolau Range of mountains that takes you from Honolulu and the leeward side of Oahu to the windward side. There's a scenic lookout at the top of the pass. It should be a must for every visitor," Ruel told her. "Would you like to go?"

"It isn't on the way home, though." Julie was positive of that.

"It isn't that far out of our way," he assured her.

"In other words, you are taking me there whether I want to go or not?" She laughed as she made the accusation.

"That's right," he admitted.

The highway that they traveled climbed toward the mountains with their steep, fluted cliffs forming a long serrated ridge. Clouds drifted near the peaks of the range.

"The Pali highway is occasionally closed," Ruel informed her. "The mountain gap sometimes focuses and concentrates the tradewinds into hurricane force. There's a morbid joke that if someone tries to commit suicide by jumping off the cliffs when these winds are blowing, he'll get blown back up. That's an exaggeration. However, the waterfalls in Nuuanu Valley on the windward side have been known to flow upside down."

"Really?" Julie was skeptical.

"It's the truth." He took the exit to the lookout and parked the car. The cities and coastline of the windward side spread out before them, the vivid blue of the ocean outlining the boundary of the island. "Here, at the Pali, is where Kamehameha the Great, the first of the Hawaiian monarchs to rule all of the Hawaiian Islands, conquered the Oahuans. He drove them up Nuuanu Valley to the Pali, and finally over the cliffs. People still find the bones of these warriors from time to time around the foot of the cliff."

Julie shuddered. It was difficult to imagine that a place so beautiful could have seen such a bloodied incident. The cliffs were steep. It was a very long way to the bottom.

"How is your geography, teacher?" Ruel asked with a mocking inflection.

"It isn't my strongest subject, but I think I'm adequate in it." She turned from the view to study him, a half-smile curving her wide mouth.

His roughly hewn features were very male—compellingly so. Her heartbeat quickened in response to the powerful attraction she felt for this man. It caught at her breath, making it shallow.

"Are you aware that the chain of Hawaiian islands consists of some of the tallest mountains in the world?" he quizzed.

"No," Julie confessed.

"The Pacific Ocean is from sixteen to eighteen thousand feet deep off of these islands. Mauna Kea on the big island is over thirteen thousand feet above the sea. From its base on the ocean floor to its peak, it's somewhere over thirty thousand feet."

"I'm impressed," she said, and meant it.

There had been a lazy glitter in the blue of his eyes. It was gone. Now there was a brooding quality to his look. Julie became aware of his right arm stretched along the back of the seat with his hand resting on the leather upholstery very near her shoulder.

With her long hair swept into a honey-colored coil, the curve of her neck was exposed. His forefinger traced the sensitive cord that ran the length of her neck. Julie's lashes fluttered closed in reaction to his deliberately sensual caress.

"You're beautiful." It was a flat statement, spoken quietly. "You have a very delectable neck."

Julie had little difficulty imagining Ruel nibbling on her skin. Her skin tingled from the feathery con-

tact of his hand, igniting the fire of longing in her
flesh. The fact kept running through her mind that
Ruel had an apartment in Honolulu. Opening her
eyes, she stared straight ahead.

"It's getting late. I think it's time we started
home." She kept her voice low, hoping it wouldn't
quiver.

"There's another full hour of sunlight left," Ruel
said. "I thought we'd drive over by Koko Head. You
haven't seen the blowhole."

"I've done enough sight-seeing for one day," Julie
insisted, unable to meet the penetrating study of his
gaze. "I'd rather go back so I have time to relax
before dinner."

"Whatever you say." The light touch of his fingertips on her neck ended as he withdrew his arm from
the back of the seat and started the car.

Retracing their route to the lookout, they rejoined
Pali Highway. Instead of returning to Honolulu,
Ruel continued across the pass. The tropical rain
forest of eucalyptus and kukui trees, thick ferns and
philodendrons was left behind on the leeward side as
the highway tunneled through the cliffs.

Ruel switched on the radio. It was tuned to a
station that played native Hawaiian songs. Julie
couldn't understand the words and had never heard
some of the melodies; but that didn't diminish her
enjoyment of the music. It was a double blessing
since it filled the silence and eliminated the need to
talk.

On previous excursions around the island, Julie
had traveled as far south on the windward side as the

Valley of the Temples. It wasn't long before she was in familiar territory. Shortly after Ruel had turned onto the Kamehameha Highway along the coastline, she saw the small, conical-shaped island, called Chinaman's Hat for obvious reasons, sitting in the bay.

Farther on, the road cut through a banana grove. The short, stocky trees with their wide fronds resembled shaggy palm trees in a constant state of molt. Heavy stocks of green bananas drooped from the fronds. After passing the Polynesian Cultural Center at Laie and the Kahuku Sugar Mill, they drove by the excavations for an aquafarm where seafood would be cultivated. Square ponds were being formed by bulldozers to raise prawns once the squares were flooded.

Rounding Kuilima Point, they were on the north shore of Oahu. It wouldn't be long before they reached the private road leading to the house. Julie stole a glance at Ruel. There was something uncompromising in the grim set of his features.

The sun had dipped so low that it was shining directly in their eyes when she looked back at the highway. Blinking at the blinding light, she covered her eyes. The car slowed to make the curve into Waimea Bay and the sun was temporarily blocked by the opposite headland. The car didn't follow the highway around the bay. Ruel turned off at the entrance to Waimea Falls.

Julie sat up. "Where are we going?"

"You said you wanted to relax before dinner. I decided we would stop here for a drink," he said, unconcerned that she hadn't been consulted.

CHAPTER NINE

ALMOST IMMEDIATELY the narrow walls of the verdant valley began closing in on them, blocking out the setting sun. The thick tropical growth kept the valley floor shaded and cool. Julie hadn't yet recovered from her surprise regarding his announcement.

Ruel quirked an eyebrow at her. "Any objections?"

"You could have asked me," she managed.

"You would have said no. I would have insisted." He shrugged. "Now it's an accomplished fact and we were both spared all that unpleasantness." The car was parked in the lot and Ruel half turned in his seat to face her. "This is a lovely, peaceful place. Do I drink alone or will you come with me?"

Obviously he was going whether she accompanied him or not, Julie realized. Which meant she could either sit in the car and wait for him or catch the bus. Both sounded slightly juvenile, and she was supposed to be an adult.

"I'll come with you," she agreed, striving to sound offhand about her decision.

"Good." A smile crinkled his tanned face and sent Julie's heart knocking against her ribs. It was directed at her only briefly as Ruel turned to open his door and step out.

Julie followed suit, not waiting for him to walk

around to open her door. Together they crossed the parking lot to the park's rustic wooden buildings. A rooster strutted out of their way—part of the wild fowl that lived in the park.

Ruel's hand rested on the back of her waist as they climbed the steps to the wooden-floored breezeway between the buildings. His touch was a warm, vital thing that seemed to spread through her. He guided her down the length of the buildings to the outdoor staircase to the second floor.

On the upstairs *lanai,* they sat at a table near the railing. It overlooked a grassy clearing where peacocks were parading, their eerie cries at odds with their beauty. The sky had turned golden and the birds began finding their favorite roosts in the tall spreading monkeypod trees.

A waiter came to their table to take their order. "May I order you a cocktail?" he asked.

Ruel glanced at Julie, saw her hesitation, and ordered, "A Blue Hawaii for the lady, and I'll have a Scotch."

"Yes, sir."

Julie opened her mouth to protest, but the waiter was gone. She looked at Ruel and saw the complacent curve of his mouth. "Don't you like Blue Hawaii?" he asked.

"I don't know. I've never had one," she answered with faint exasperation.

"I thought you'd like to try one of our exotic drinks. The Mai Tai and Chi Chi are very popular, too, but you seemed more the Blue Hawaii type. If you don't like it, you can order something else." He seemed to dismiss her objection with arrogant ease.

"Thank you," she acknowledged with biting mockery.

Amusement lurked in the blue depths of his eyes at her response, but he made no comment. The waiter returned and set a tall, stemmed glass in front of Julie. The liquid inside the glass was a vivid blue, topped with a wedge of pineapple and a maraschino cherry. Julie sipped at the drink through a straw. It was sweet, but not overly so, and tasted deceptively innocuous.

"How do you like it?" Ruel asked.

"It's good," she admitted. "What's in it?"

"Rum and pineapple juice with blue Curaçao." He named the ingredients. "Are you sorry we stopped here?"

"No." Julie wasn't sure what she was admitting when she said that, but it was the truth. The setting was serenely beautiful with dusk stealing gently over the valley. From the open *lanai*, Julie saw the glimmering light of the evening star.

"I thought this place would appeal to you after spending your day in those musty, dusty museums," said Ruel.

"The museums were neither musty nor dusty," Julie corrected, although she knew he was only teasing. "I'm still surprised that you went to so much trouble to find me."

"Are you surprised?" came his quiet challenge.

She struggled to ignore the implication of his question. "I appreciate the effort you made to find me." She sipped at her drink and swirled the blue liquid. "I didn't expect the ride home."

"I didn't suggest it this morning because I didn't know what time I would be finished with my appointments today," Ruel explained. "And because I thought you would dream up some excuse not to accept."

Julie thought he was probably right and tried to defend herself. "Simply because I don't expect you to act as my chauffeur."

"Is that the reason?" His mouth quirked dryly. "I thought it was my company you were seeking to avoid." He signaled the waiter to come to their table, then glanced at Julie. "In that case, will you have dinner with me? The food here is very good." The waiter arrived before Julie could respond. "We'd like to look at your menu now," Ruel requested.

"Yes, sir."

As the waiter walked away, Julie protested, "We can't stay for dinner. It's getting late."

Darkness had settled quickly in the valley. She couldn't even make out the shapes of the peacocks nesting in the trees. Their table was lit by a candle flame protected by a colored glass container.

"Do you have a date this evening?" Ruel took the menus the waiter handed him and passed one to Julie.

Automatically she reached for it. "I don't have a date," she admitted, "but your aunt will be expecting me."

"You have all day Saturdays and Sundays off.

Why should she be expecting you?" He opened his menu and began looking at the fare.

"But I'm always back in time for dinner," she told him. "Emily will be worried if I'm not there by seven."

He gave her a disconcerting look and reached in his slack's pocket. There was a jingle of coins, then he was placing a quarter on the table in front of Julie.

"There's a telephone downstairs. Call her and tell her you won't be back for dinner tonight." The directness of his gaze challenged her to come up with another excuse.

Julie didn't try. Her fingers hesitantly closed around the shiny coin. It was still warm from his body heat. She looked at it for several seconds, then lifted her gaze to his.

"Shall I tell her not to expect you, either?" she challenged, but that wasn't the question she was really asking.

"I'm a grown man. I don't have to report in," he informed her with cynical mockery.

"Excuse me, then," she muttered, her jaw tightening in resentment of his attitude.

She avoided looking at him as she pushed her chair away from the table and rose. Ruel made the courteous pretense of rising. Pride wanted to make Julie change her mind about having dinner with him, but she had already more or less accepted his invitation. To refuse now would invite questions from him that she didn't want to answer.

Descending the stairs, she walked to the public

telephone and deposited the coin. She dialed the number and listened to the ringing on the other end of the line. On the third ring it was answered by Emily.

"This is Julie," she identified herself.

"Julie—I was just wondering where you were." The woman confirmed what Julie suspected.

"I thought I'd better call to let you know I won't be there for dinner," she said.

"Oh." The one word was followed by a long pause. "Will you be home very late tonight?"

"No." Julie glanced toward the staircase to the *lanai* where Ruel waited. "No, I don't expect to be late." Since Emily hadn't asked, she didn't volunteer the information as to whom she was with.

"Very well. Enjoy yourself."

She wasn't sure if she wanted to do that. "Thank you, I will. Good night." She rang off.

When she returned to the *lanai,* Ruel stood and held out her chair, pushing it forward after she sat down. Seating himself, he ran his alert gaze over her face.

"Did you speak to Em?" he asked.

"Yes." A fresh drink was sitting beside her half-empty glass. "I didn't order another one."

"I ordered it for you." He leaned back in his chair, looking so laid back and casual. "Is Em satisfied that you're safe?"

Julie hesitated and sipped at her first drink. "Yes, she's satisfied, I think," she answered finally.

"Did you tell her you were with me?" he questioned, and she could almost feel his gaze narrow on her.

"No."

"Why?"

"Because I thought you didn't want her to know." Julie shrugged briefly, glancing at him.

"Why should I care whether or not she knows? She isn't likely to object. What made you think I didn't want her to know?" Ruel questioned.

"I don't know. Probably because of your policy of noninvolvement with the hired help," she retorted defensively.

"Circumstances sometimes require policies to be changed." His curt response was punctuated by the clinking of ice cubes as he lifted the glass of Scotch to his lips.

"What kind of circumstances?" Julie challenged, wanting him to feel as uncomfortable as she did.

"Like not being able to forget what it was like to hold you in my arms," answered Ruel without hesitation.

Her lungs seemed to stop functioning, neither breathing in nor exhaling air. She stared at her drink, unable to look at him yet riveted by the blue color of the liquid, its shade not that different from the arresting blue of his eyes. Her heart pounded in her throat.

"No comment?" Ruel taunted.

"No." She swallowed to ease the tightness in her throat and nervously smoothed one side of her hair back to its coil. "No comment." She was a poor liar.

She never would have been able to convince him she had forgotten what it was like.

"Would you prefer to dine inside or out here?" His change of subject was a godsend for Julie.

"Inside," she chose, hoping the well-lit interior of the restaurant would dispel the feeling of intimacy the darkened *lanai* projected.

Rising, he took her fresh drink. "Leave it," he said of the first one. "The ice has diluted its flavor by now."

Julie didn't argue. The last sip had been very watery. She walked through the wide opening into the restaurant while Ruel followed, carrying their drinks. She paused inside the after-ceilinged room with its planked walls and board floor. Its turn-of-the-century motif was achieved with stained glass and expensive antiques.

"California! What are you doing here?" The enthusiastic greeting from Frank Smith brought Julie's gaze around in surprise.

He came hustling toward her, his boyish handsome face wreathed in a smile. Neatly dressed in dark trousers, a white shirt and a print vest, his appearance made her guess that this was the restaurant where he worked.

"Hello, Frank." Conscious of Ruel behind her, Julie's greeting was much more subdued. She had a vague feeling of dread. She wished now that she had been interested enough to ask Frank where he worked before now.

"Why didn't you let me know you were coming?"

Frank stopped in front of her, his eyes seeing only her.

"I didn't know," she answered truthfully, and would have drawn his attention to Ruel, but Frank didn't give her a chance.

"Listen, I have to work until closing, but we'll be having a combo here to entertain in a little bit. Maybe you can stay——"

"The lady is with me." Ruel towered beside her. "And we won't be staying to hear the combo."

Frank's head jerked toward him. He glanced from Ruel to Julie and back to Ruel again. He looked pale beneath his dark tan and there was the thinness of anger to his lips.

"I didn't realize Julie was with you, Mr. Chandler." It was more a challenge than an apology.

"Obviously," was Ruel's dry response. "You will excuse us."

Frank stepped aside, flashing Julie a look that demanded to know what she was doing with Ruel. An answer was impossible under the circumstances. The host came forward and led them to a booth. Its floor-to-ceiling partition guaranteed privacy for its occupants. Sitting on the thickly cushioned booth seat, Julie glanced across the table at Ruel.

"I didn't know Frank worked here," she said, just in case he thought she did.

"Neither did I," he retorted. If he had, Julie guessed he would have chosen another restaurant.

"Good evening." Frank appeared at their table, his expression polite, regarding them as strangers. Julie whitened as she realized he was to serve their table. "Both the *mahimahi* and *opakapaka* are fresh this evening. The pork ribs are always excellent." He filled their goblets with ice water. "Would you care to see the wine list, sir?"

"No, thank you." Irritation darkened Ruel's eyes to the color of deep water.

"I'll be back in a few minutes to take your order," Frank nodded, and moved away.

Julie glanced at Ruel, expecting a comment, but he made none. The menu was in front of her. She opened it, not having looked at it when she was on the *lanai.* There was a full range of dishes from glazed mandarin duck to prime rib.

"What would you like?" Ruel asked.

"I don't know." She couldn't decide. "What is this Hawaiian platter like?" It contained a combination of Hawaiian foods.

"Have you eaten any Hawaiian dishes?" Ruel asked.

"Only what Malia has fixed," Julie admitted. "What's *lomi lomi* salmon? Or this *kalua* pig?"

"The *lomi lomi* salmon is raw salmon that's been massaged for tenderness." His mouth quirked at the slight face she made. "The *kalua* pig is pork that's probably been baked in an earth oven. I wouldn't recommend that you try the Hawaiian platter. The food is an acquired taste, especially the *poi,* which is a starchy vegetable, like a potato, that's been pounded into a pulp, diluted with water, and allowed to ferment."

"You're right. I think I'll pass up the Hawaiian

platter," she agreed with a decisive nod. "What do you recommend?"

"Do you like fish?"

"Yes, but I've already had *mahimahi*. I'd like to try something different." Julie studied the menu.

"Why not have the *opakapaka?*" Ruel suggested.

"What is it?" She was wary after his last explanation.

"Red snapper," he smiled.

"I'll have that," she decided immediately, and joined in when Ruel chuckled softly.

The moment of shared laughter ended the instant Frank returned. Ruel gave him their order in a precise, clipped tone. He remained aloof and vaguely brooding after Frank left. Conversation became difficult and strained. His responses were often cynical and taunting, and the situation wasn't helped by the way Frank kept checking their table to be certain everything was all right. Julie suspected that he was deliberately trying to spoil their evening.

"Shall I take your plate, sir?" Frank appeared the minute Ruel had finished. At an affirmative nod, he gathered the plate and silverware. "More coffee, sir? Dessert?"

"Nothing right now." Ruel flashed him a dismissing look.

"You may take my plate, Frank. I'm through," Julie told him. He stacked her dishes on the tray with Ruel's. Before Frank could inquire, she added, "Nothing more for me."

As Frank carried the dishes away, Ruel offered her a cigarette, but she shook her head in silent refusal. Ruel took one for himself. There was a hint of impatience in the way he snapped the lighter and brought the flame to the cigarette and clicked the gold lid shut.

"Your boyfriend is making a jealous pest of himself." He breathed out a stream of gray smoke.

"It isn't my fault," Julie replied.

"Meaning it's mine?" he challenged.

"Meaning it's his. I have no control over the way he behaved, any more than you would if it were one of your girl friends who was waiting on us," she reasoned.

A cold smile twitched the corners of his mouth. "They probably wouldn't be so civilized about it."

He appeared to be fascinated by the smoke curling from the end of his cigarette. Julie studied him. His expression seemed grimly rueful and cynical. Had it been because of the reference to his girl friends? Why had she put it in the plural? Why did she assume he wouldn't be satisfied with one girl? Because he was still unmarried? How had he escaped for so long?

"Why haven't you married, Ruel?" she asked boldly, wanting to know the answer.

"Maybe," he slowly lifted his gaze to hers, "because I haven't found a woman who didn't bore me either out of bed or in it." His voice was as serious as his expression. With a sinking heart, Julie was forced to believe what he said.

"Your check, sir." Frank placed a small tray on the table beside Ruel and began refilling the water goblets.

After glancing at the amount, Ruel placed a bill on the tray. "Keep the change."

"Thank you, sir." Frank picked up the tray with the money.

Each time Frank said "sir" in that ingratiating way, Julie saw Ruel's jaw tighten. His irritation was turning into an anger that tested his control. It lurked in the sharpness of his gaze as it sliced across the table to her.

"Are you ready to leave?" It was meant to be a polite inquiry, but it was a little too abrupt for that.

Julie agreed without delay. To get to the stairs, they had to pass the cash register. Frank was there, and his gaze sought Julie as they approached. She held her breath, hoping he wouldn't say any more to Ruel. Frank didn't, but the host who was behind the cash register did.

"Good evening, Mr. Chandler. I hope everything was satisfactory tonight."

The inquiry forced Ruel to slow his stride to respond. When he did, Frank was at Julie's side. She tried to warn him away with a shake of her head, but he paid no attention.

As Ruel said, "It was fine, thank you," to the host, Frank was whispering a demanding, "Will I see you tomorrow at the beach, Julie?"

Before she could draw a breath, Ruel was clamping a hand on her elbow. "No, you will not!" he snapped at Frank, and propelled her toward the staircase.

"You don't own her, mister!" Frank hurled after him.

By then they were halfway down the first flight of steps. "What did you mean telling Frank that?" Julie demanded, her temper flaring.

"Exactly what I said." They had reached the ground floor and Ruel directed her toward the parking lot. His iron grip of her elbow didn't permit her to slow down.

"Sunday happens to be my day off, as you pointed out earlier this evening," she reminded. "I may do what I please and see whom I please."

"You aren't going to see that punk kid," Ruel stated.

"I won't be told what I may do. Not by you or anybody!" Julie retorted.

He flashed her an angry look and unlocked the passenger door of the car. He more or less pushed her inside and slammed the door. This time his high-handed tactics had gone a little too far. Julie sat in the richly upholstered leather seats and fumed.

Without addressing another word to her, Ruel slid behind the wheel and started the motor. The sleek sports car had been built for speed, maneuverability and acceleration. As the car roared out of the parking lot onto the curving drive to the highway, Ruel seemed intent on testing all three.

The powerful thrust of the engine pushed Julie's shoulders against the back of the seat. At the junction with the highway, the car made a running stop before turning onto the road that was miraculously free of traffic at that moment.

The tires squealed around the corner and spun at the sudden demand for acceleration. The speed that they were traveling had Julie's heart in her throat. They were racing in the opposite direction to the house, but it seemed of little importance.

Traversing the twisting, curving highway that followed the coastline, weaving in and out of traffic, they covered large chunks of ground in record time. Julie's gaze was riveted to the road directly ahead of them, illuminated by their headlights. Any second she expected them to miss a turn or overshoot a curve.

Once she forced a look at Ruel. The strong hands on the steering wheel seemed totally in control—firm in their grip yet relaxed. There was nothing in Ruel's expression to indicate that he thought they were going unduly fast. Neither was there anger. But a glimpse at the speedometer made Julie close her eyes.

It never once occurred to her to say something to Ruel, not even to suggest that he slow down. Possibly she didn't want to distract his steel-blue gaze from the road. It was worse riding with her eyes closed. She couldn't see what was going to happen next. She opened them just as Ruel swept past a slower car.

Suddenly she was staring into an oncoming pair of headlights, and she breathed in a stifled cry. She understood what Emily had said about how dangerously fast Ruel drove. The black sports car swerved easily into its own lane, missing the oncoming car by several yards.

Almost immediately its speed began to decrease. Taking the first really safe breath she'd drawn since leaving the restaurant parking lot, Julie glanced at Ruel.

"I'm sorry, I didn't mean to frighten you," he apologized, flicking her a brief glance.

"It's okay." But her voice sounded shaky.

The shoulder of the highway widened to provide parking on the beach side of the road. Ruel slowed the car and turned onto the shoulder. Switching off the motor, he looked out of the front screen at the ocean. A thin strip of sandy beach was in front of the car. Julie had no idea where they were nor how far they had come.

"I'm going for a short walk on the beach," Ruel announced, and opened his door. "You're welcome to come along if you want."

The invitation was so offhand that Julie wasn't certain if he meant it. It didn't matter to her. A walk, better yet a stroll, was as fast as she wanted to travel for a while. And she liked the idea of having land under her feet.

When she climbed out of her side of the car, Ruel was already standing on the ribbon of pale sand at the water's edge. His hands were thrust deep in his pockets. Closing the door, Julie walked over the dune. The coolness of the tradewinds seemed to fill her lungs, reviving her.

As she walked onto the beach, her shoes sank into the sand. Granules trickled inside, and she stopped. Balancing on one foot, she took off one shoe, then the other, and carried them in her hand. Barefoot, she walked down to where the waves lapped the

shore. At night, with only the moon and stars for
light, the water seemed to shine.

Farther along the coast, the strip of beach widened. A grove of windswept ironwoods rose on its
dunes. Julie wandered in their general direction,
aware that Ruel had begun to stroll after her. She
lifted her face to the sea air, feeling it wash away her
tension.

CHAPTER TEN

THE WAVES were stronger near the stand of iron-woods. They crashed onto and over the lava rocks that edged the sand at the shore. Julie stopped to watch the churning white foam lift, plunge and recede. She heard the crunch of Ruel's footsteps in the sand directly behind her.

"It's quite a sight, isn't it?" she said over her shoulder, her gaze not straying from the pounding surf.

"Yes," was his one-word agreement, issued in a calm but absent voice.

He had stopped closer to her than Julie had first realized. Still she didn't turn from the mesmerizing sight of the sea. Something seemed to slip from her hair, but not until the sensation was repeated did she realize that the pins securing the coiled bun at the nape of her neck were being pulled out of her hair.

Letting her shoes fall to the ground, she turned. "Don't do that!" she protested impatiently, and lifted her hands to try to repair the damage.

Ruel ignored her and continued to pull out the hairpins, despite her effort to stop him. In a matter of seconds her hair was tumbling about her shoulders as she was powerless to do anything about it.

"Why did you do that?" she sighed in exasperation.

"I like it better this way," Ruel answered. He slid

his fingers into the tangled silk of her hair and cupped her head in both of his hands. "I've wanted to do that ever since I saw you at the breakfast table this morning. That hairdo reminds me of a prim and proper——"

"Schoolteacher," Julie provided the comparison.

Her face was tilted toward his while her heart raced faster than the sports car had. His hands were so strong, yet so devastatingly gentle. His shadowed eyes seemed to be taking in every detail of her face.

"Yes, a schoolteacher," he agreed and, with a low groan, he was covering her mouth with his.

There was no holding back, and Julie didn't try. She wound her arms around his middle and pressed herself close to his length. The hard, branding kiss seemed to burn itself into her very soul. Ruel wasn't content to take possession of only her lips. Holding her face in his hands, he kissed every inch of it before reclaiming the softness of her lips.

Releasing her face, he slid his arms around her and gathered her into the fullness of his embrace. Desire quaked through her and erupted to flow like fire through her veins. Ecstasy burned in its wake as she felt the way Ruel trembled against her, disturbed as greatly as she was.

Her hands slipped under the hem of his shirt, seeking to feel the bareness of his hard flesh. It was hot to the touch, as hot as the flames that burned inside them both. The skin of his back was stretched tautly over his hard muscles.

He abandoned her mouth to explore the curve of her neck, nibbling at the sensitive skin. The caress of his hands was creating new needs within her. All her senses were dominated by him. He murmured her name over and over again in hungry demand.

When she felt his fingers loosening the buttons of her blouse, she helped him. Ruel left the task to her and unfastened the front closing of her bra. Then his hands were taking her over. But Julie had never felt so deliriously happy in all her life. The bruising force of his kiss was pure bliss. The light caress of his hands was sweet torture. They were wrapped in each other's arms and it still wasn't close enough for either of them.

Suddenly something drove at their legs, undermining the sand beneath their feet. Ruel staggered forward a step carrying Julie with him, almost completely losing his balance for a moment. Dazed, she opened her eyes to see a wave receding to the ocean. An object bobbed on its surface.

"My shoes!" she gasped.

Ruel had been as slow to recover and identify the cause as she had been. The puzzled frown that creased his forehead indicated that he didn't understand why she should be concerned about her shoes.

"I dropped them on the sand, and the wave is taking them away—the one that hit us," she explained as she tugged at the arm around her waist holding her captive.

Glancing over his shoulder, Ruel started to let go of her and then held her back. "Stay here, I'll get them." But as he waded into the water, another wave swelled into a curl that drove him back to shore.

When it receded, Julie could no longer see her shoes. "They're gone," she whispered in disbelief.

"I'm afraid so," Ruel nodded.

She looked at him. His shoes were soaked and his pants were drenched to a point above his knees. Her shoes had been washed out to sea and the legs of her own slacks were wet with seawater. The situation took on a humorous aspect and she started to laugh.

"So you think it's funny?" Ruel challenged, smiling at her breathless laughter. His arms circled her waist to lock his hands behind her back. He drew her hips against his.

"It is," she insisted. "You, with squishy shoes and wet pant legs—me, with wet slacks and no shoes."

Despite the half-smile on his mouth, his eyes were serious in their regard of her. "You should be glad it happened."

"Why?" She shook her head, not understanding.

"It was nature's way of sousing us with cold water and putting out the hot fire," he explained calmly.

Julie sobered. Suddenly aware of the gaping front of her blouse, she pulled it shut with her hands, clutching the ends together. She made no attempt to escape the circle of his arms, but she wasn't totally at ease anymore.

"You're right." Her gaze ricocheted off his face, not able to match the steadiness of his look.

"I want you, Julie," he told her in a remarkably cool tone. "A dose of cold water hasn't changed that." He smoothed the hair away from her cheek and rested his hand along the side of her neck, strok-ing her jaw with his thumb. "I want to make love to you," he elaborated. A few minutes ago, their mutual cravings would have been satisfied.

"Here's your chance for second thoughts," he told her. "Your one and only chance to have the wisdom of hindsight. I have an apartment in Honolulu. No waves will come crashing in there. Will you go there with me?"

"Wh-What about your policy?" she faltered.

"Policy be damned! I want you, Julie." His voice was low and urgent, controlled but only barely.

Instead of feeling joy at his words, Julie felt chilled. Everything began to freeze up inside her. "Aren't you worried that I might bore you?" It came out flat and cold.

A grim anger hardened his features. A muscle flexed in his arm as if he meant to crush her to his chest and drive that coolness from her body. After a long second, he let her go and took a step away.

"Let's go back to the car so I can drive you home," he said.

Her mind seemed incapable of focusing on anything of substance. Only little things registered as they walked silently and apart to the car. Unimportant things like buying a new pair of shoes to replace the ones she lost, and wondering where Ruel had discarded the pins he had taken from her hair. In the car, Julie thought about the sand they were tracking onto the carpeted floorboards and wondered if the seawater from their wet pant legs would damage the upholstery of the seats.

The lights were on downstairs when they reached the house. Julie had no conception of the time—

whether it was late or early. The gravel in the driveway bit into the bare soles of her feet as she stepped from the car and she had to pick her way to the steps. Ruel reached the front door ahead of her and opened it for her.

Emily Harmon was coming down the stairs as Julie entered the large foyer. "You're home, Julie. I was wondering what time to expect you." Her smile of greeting contained relief. When she saw Ruel walk in behind Julie, her eyes widened in surprise. "You didn't tell me you were with Ruel."

"Didn't I? I thought I had." Julie tossed out the lie with numbed unconcern.

"Where are your shoes?" Emily began to take in the appearance of both of them, a thousand puzzled questions leaping into her eyes.

"I took them off to walk on the beach and a wave washed them out to sea. Ruel waded in after them, but he couldn't reach them." Julie felt something begin to splinter inside of her and knew she couldn't keep answering these questions. "Excuse me, Emily, I'm really a mess. I'll see you in the morning."

She rushed past the woman and up the stairs, leaving Ruel to make any more explanations that might be required by his aunt. In the safety of her room, she began shaking uncontrollably, her reaction to what had happened vibrating through her. It took all her effort to undress, wash and climb into bed.

SUNDAY CAME and went with Julie venturing no farther from the house than the swimming pool.

There were no more questions from Emily about the previous night. And Ruel was nowhere around. Those two factors should have made it easier; but instead the tension mounted within her.

Mid-afternoon on Monday, Julie was in Debbie's room trying to explain the solution to an algebra problem. "I just don't understand how to do it. Can't we leave it for today?" Debbie pleaded. "I can't concentrate."

"I noticed," Julie sighed with short patience.

"Did Auntie Em tell you the news?" Debbie's eyes glowed with excitement, making her look closer to fourteen than seventeen.

"What news?" Julie asked the expected question.

"I'm going into the hospital on Thursday. They're going to X-ray and see how I'm healing. If everything's all right, they'll take off this cast and put me in a smaller one. I might even be able to use a wheelchair. Isn't that glorious?" she burst out.

"It certainly is," Julie agreed with a wide smile. "It's the best news I've heard in ages. I'm happy for you."

"I'm happy for me, too," Debbie declared, and glanced toward the window at the sound of a car pulling into the drive. "That's Ruel—I'd recognize his car anywhere. He's home early today. I can hardly wait to tell him, Julie!"

Blinded by her happiness, Debbie didn't see the tenseness enter Julie's features. The curve of her lips became strained. At the slam of the car door, she clenched her teeth to keep from wincing.

"You'll have to wait for a little while, because we

still have schoolwork to finish," she insisted, and tried to close her ears to the sound of the front door opening and closing.

"Not that algebra problem again!" Debbie protested in a half plea.

"It isn't so difficult."

"That's easy for you to say," Debbie sighed ruefully, and looked past Julie to the door. She broke into an immediate smile. "Hi Ruel!"

Julie stiffened, her nerve ends screaming out their awareness of his presence in the room. She refused to turn and look at him, staring instead at the equation in her hand.

"Hi, Deb. How are you?" His footsteps approached her chair by his sister's bed.

"Fine, I——"

Julie broke in, her spine rigid. "Would you mind visiting your sister after she's finished her lessons?" she demanded, indifferent to the astonished look she received from Debbie.

"I came to speak to you," Ruel stated.

He was standing much too close to her chair. In agitation, she rose and put distance between them, clasping the math papers in front of her as if they offered protection.

"As you can see, I'm busy." Briefly she let her eyes meet his narrowed gaze before she turned her head away, keeping her chin high. His hard vitality made her feel drained and vulnerable.

"This will only take a moment," he challenged.

Julie didn't trust herself alone with him. "Why would you possibly need to speak to me?" She at-

tempted to laugh away his request, but the sound
was brittle and harsh.

"For one thing," he crossed the room to where
she stood, a muscle in his jaw working convulsively,
"I wanted to give you this."

There was no place for Julie to retreat. She
couldn't keep running from him anyway. She stared
at the package he offered to her.

"What is it?" She made no move to take it.

"A pair of shoes to replace the ones you lost the
other night."

"That wasn't your responsibility. The fault was
mine for leaving them on the sand," she rejected
stiffly, and started to turn away.

"Dammit, Julie!" Ruel cursed beneath his breath,
the words barely audible, and caught at her arm
with his hand. She recoiled from his touch, an in-
stinctive reaction to keep from turning into his arms.
He compressed his mouth into a tightly grim line.
"Will you take this?" His dangerously low voice
seemed to threaten violence if she refused.

Julie took the package. "Thank you." She lifted
her gaze to his face, schooling it to look on him
impersonally. "Was there anything else, Mr. Chandler?"

"No!" The negative came out in a savage rush of
breath. "Nothing else, Miss Lancaster." Sarcastical-
ly Ruel flung her formality back in her face. Turning, he nodded curtly to Debbie. "I'll be in to see you
later." He didn't wait for a response as he let his long
strides carry him from the room.

"What was that all about?" Debbie queried, her speculative gaze examining Julie.

"Your brother brought me some shoes to replace a pair I lost, that's all." Julie tried to make light of the incident, walking around the bed to set the package on a side table.

"I know all about your lost shoes. I heard you come home Saturday night—with Ruel. After you went upstairs, he told Em that you two had dinner together." Debbie continued to study her intently. Julie found the look in the girl's eye was much too worldly and knowing. "What happened? Did you two have an argument?"

"Why would I be arguing with your brother?" Julie dodged the question with a stilted laugh.

"Listen, a minute ago the air in here was so thick, you needed a machete to cut through it," Debbie declared.

"That's nonsense. You're imagining things," Julie insisted, and began shuffling papers in a show of business.

"I don't think so. For instance, I know Ruel didn't take you to dinner Saturday night just so you could have a meal out. He took you because you're a woman. You went because he's a man."

"Debbie——" Julie began.

"Don't bother to deny it." Debbie didn't give Julie a chance to finish her sentence. "It's the most natural thing in the world—the two of you living under the same roof, eating breakfast and dinner together. Ruel is bound to have noticed you. And nobody can ignore him for long. You've fallen for him, haven't you?"

"No!" It was a sharp, explosive denial and an outright lie.

"It's okay, Julie," Debbie consoled. "Everybody does."

"Thanks!" It wasn't any comfort to know she was one of the many.

"I'm sorry. Maybe you'll feel better if you tell me what you fought about?" Debbie suggested.

"Once and for all, Debbie, we didn't fight." It had been a clear-cut parting of the ways. "I'm not going to discuss your brother any further. Is that clear?"

"I was just trying to help." Debbie's dark eyes held a look of wounded dignity.

"You can help by getting on with your lessons," Julie retorted.

BY THE TIME Thursday arrived, Julie was almost glad to see Debbie leave for the hospital, since it gave her a respite from the girl's scrutiny. At almost seventeen, Debbie was too perceptive. She didn't make any more attempts to invite Julie's confidence, but it was unspoken in her every look, and the strain of ignoring it had begun to wear her nerves thin. It had been as difficult to endure as Ruel's studied politeness, so cool and aloof.

Julie wasn't on hand to welcome Debbie home late Friday afternoon. She had swum in the pool to the point of exhaustion and was stretched out on one of the lounge chairs when she heard the commotion that heralded Debbie's return. She didn't think she could match the happy sound of the voices filtering from the house, so she made no attempt to join them. Besides, Ruel would be there and Julie preferred not to be with Debbie when he was around and vice versa.

Closing her eyes to the glaring angle of the sun, she tried to relax. Its warmth couldn't ease the tension that stiffened her muscles and frayed at her nerves. She was living each day as it came, never asking herself how long she could stand up under the strain.

The familiar slip-slipping sound of Malia's thongs on the sun deck warned her of the housekeeper's approach. "Miss Emily was wondering where you were, Julie. Debbie has come home from the hospital."

"Yes, I heard." She didn't move nor open her eyes.

"You should see her! She's so excited about that wheelchair," Malia declared. "It will be good for her to be able to get out of that room for a little while each day."

"Yes, it certainly will," Julie agreed. "Debbie has been looking forward to that."

"Yes, she has. Aren't you going to come in to see her?" Malia asked when Julie showed no indication of leaving the pool area.

"Later," promised Julie, "after the initial excitement of coming home has died down. Besides, I know . . . her brother and Emily will want to spend some time with her, and I wouldn't want to intrude."

"Miss Emily wouldn't think you were intruding," Malia replied. "And Ruel has a dinner engagement in town this evening. He said he just had time to shower and change before he leaves."

"Oh." Julie swallowed at the lump that rose in her throat. His dinner companion would probably be some beautiful woman who didn't care if she bored him. "Tell Debbie I'll be in to see her later," she repeated at last. "Sometime before dinner."

"I will." There was a faint sigh in Malia's voice as if she regretted not being able to persuade Julie to come in sooner.

As Julie listened to the woman's footsteps retreating to the house, she felt a tear trickle out of the corner of her eye and into her hair.

She wiped it away with a finger. Opening her eyes, she tried to blink away the moistness that was gathering in them. Her throat ached and it hurt to breathe.

Something—a sound or a sensation—made her look up. Ruel was standing on the *lanai* overlooking the pool. The doors of his bedroom were open behind him. His shirt was pulled free of the waistband of his trousers and was unbuttoned three-quarters of the way down; he looked as if he had been halted in the act of taking it off. He was staring at her, stretched out on the lounge chair like a sacrificial offering to the sun.

The scanty covering of the orange bikini had never bothered Julie before, but now she felt exposed— naked. She had the feeling he could see all the way into her soul. She couldn't let him do that. Rising abruptly, she grabbed for her beach jacket and hurriedly stuffed her arms in its sleeves. She wrapped it across her front and tied the terry cloth sash. When she glanced to the upper *lanai* where Ruel had been watching, he wasn't there. The doors to his bedroom were partially shut.

Her shoulders sagged with defeat and a long, broken sigh came from her throat. What had she been protecting? Or had she merely been tilting at windmills? She concluded that she was her own worst enemy. She had to get control of herself and her emotions.

As she climbed the outer staircase to the *lanai* and her bedroom, she felt as fragile as glass. She was on the verge of breaking. The slightest jar would be capable of shattering her. She wanted to cry, but she was afraid of doing even that.

Pushing open the French doors to her room, she walked in. Her hair was almost dry from the swim, but it was matted about her shoulders. She lifted it away from her neck and let it fall back. Her appearance had ceased to concern her. Untying her beach jacket, she took it off and started to toss it on the chair by the wall. Something skittered across white-painted drywall and startled a shriek of alarm from her before she recognized the tiny harmless lizard, one of many that inhabited the gardens outdoors.

If she hadn't been so edgy, the little creature would not have scared her. Shaking in reaction, she clutched the robe to her stomach. Her heart was attempting to resume its normal beat.

"You're cracking up!" She whispered the warning to herself.

The French doors burst open. Her nerves had barely recovered from her previous fright, and she spun around, shattered to find Ruel standing inside, naked to the waist, concern etched in his hard male features.

"What is it? I heard you scream," he demanded.

She fought the rising tide of panic. "It was nothing. One of those . . . lizards or chameleons, whatever they are . . . ran across the wall," she explained in a faltering voice. "It . . . scared me for a second before I saw what it was."

Exhaling a breath, he relaxed. His muscles seemed to visibly uncoil. "You're all right, then. I thought you might have hurt yourself somehow," he said grimly.

She shook her head. "No, I'm all right."

It was impossible to tear her gaze from him. She had never seen him like this, his chest bared, hard flesh gleaming in a ripple of muscle, his skin deeply tanned all over. His virility shook her senses, assaulting her from every direction.

Her fingers curled into her palms, wanting to thread themselves through that cloud of golden-brown hair on his chest. She could almost hear the steady pounding of his heart—or was it hers? The male scent of him seemed to reach across the room and envelop her.

Ruel seemed so primitive standing there, half-dressed. The sight of him touched a similar core in her own being. She looked into his face and saw his gaze waywardly working its way over her bikini-clad torso. The beach jacket was a crumpled ball, pressed to her stomach, concealing none of her curves.

When his eyes met hers she saw the desire blazing there, and elemental hunger trembled through her. She felt raw and exposed, defenseless against him, because of the uncontrollable emotion he aroused.

"Get out of my bedroom." It was a hoarse plea not to test her resistance any farther. She knew she had none.

His head made a short, negative movement. "Julie." He held out a hand in silent entreaty and took a step toward her.

With a half-muffled cry she swayed toward him. It was all the answer Ruel needed as he crossed the room to sweep her into his arms. Julie locked her arms around his neck, her toes dangling off the floor. The dam had burst and nothing could hold back the tide of her love.

CHAPTER ELEVEN

HALF-SOBBING WITH JOY, she pressed kisses against his jaw and cheek while he buried his mouth in the curve of her neck. "I don't care anymore."

"Julie," he moaned.

His trembling lips moved up her neck to seek the parted softness of hers. His sighing breath of satisfaction filled her mouth with a quaking intimacy. She felt his hand moving up her spine to the halter bow of her bikini. A pull of the string and it loosened. She hunched her shoulders so he could remove the top completely, then it went sailing across the room as naked flesh met naked flesh.

"God, how I've wanted you," Ruel muttered against the hollow of her throat.

Unburdened by her weight, he carried her to the bed and laid her on the coverlet. The mattress sagged as he followed her down. With the pressure of his body spread half over her and half beside her, Julie's limbs felt curiously weak. A heady lethargy took hold of her and she surrendered to the sensuous demands he made.

She shuddered with desire when he bent to kiss the curve of her breast and tease the rosy peak into hardness. The sensual ache for fulfilment warmed her body—and she was overwhelmingly aware that Ruel was equally disturbed.

His mouth was back on her lips, crushing them,

nibbling their edges. *"Kulie."* The golden cloud of
chest hairs settled onto her rosy peaks. His hand slid
down her waist, closing over her hipbone. *"Ipo,
ku'uipo,"* he murmured into her mouth. *"Aloha auia
oe."* He rubbed his chin and cheek against hers in a
rough caress. His eyes were half-closed, smoldering
over her in passion. "I don't know why it comes out
so much easier in Hawaiian," he said thickly. "Do
you know what I said?"

"No." Words had ceased to matter. They were
after all only words. "Kiss me. Love me, Ruel," she
begged.

His mouth covered hers in urgent possession. His
hands were seeking and shaping her curves to him.
Neither could seem to get close enough to the other.
His weight crushing her more fully onto the bed; his
body rising above her.

A succession of sharp raps on the door was followed immediately by Emily calling, "Julie? Are
you all right?"

Julie surfaced from his kiss with a rush, but not
quickly enough to call out an answer. The knob
rattled as she searched for her voice. The door
opened and Emily stepped in.

It all happened in a span of seconds. There wasn't
sufficient time for Julie and Ruel to separate. After
Julie's initial glimpse of Emily's shocked expression,
she turned her face away, burying it in the hard
muscle of his upper arm. He shielded her from his
aunt's view for a moment.

"What is going on here?" Emily finally breathed
out the demand.

"Dammit! What the hell do you think is going on?" Ruel snapped, and levered himself away from Julie to rise from the bed.

Hot with shame and embarrassment, Julie rolled onto her side, grabbing for the edge of the coverlet to hide her nakedness. Waves of nausea swamped her. She thought she was going to be sick. She couldn't bring herself to look at either Emily or Ruel.

"Julie, I——" The shock of disappointment and disapproval was in the woman's voice.

"For God's sake, Em, leave her alone," he muttered.

"You know very well that I will not permit such goings on in this house, Ruel," his aunt declared, provoked into rage.

"Leave Julie alone! If anyone needs to be lectured, it's me." The anger in his voice was barely controlled.

Silent sobs began to shake Julie's shoulders. Her trembling fingers pulled the coverlet closer around her; she hunched her shoulders beneath it. Despite what Ruel said, she knew she was as much to blame for what happened as he was.

A hand touched her shoulder and she cringed from it. Her tear-filled eyes were aware of Ruel standing beside her, but she couldn't turn to him. He hesitated.

"It was my fault. I'll explain to Em," he promised quietly. "Julie, I have to go now."

She couldn't lift her head to look at him. She wasn't sure if she could look at anyone in the face again. She simply nodded that she had heard what he said as she drowned in her private sea of misery.

She heard him walk to the door. When it closed, she slumped onto the bed, tortured sobs racking her body. It had all seemed so beautiful and right, and now it had become sordid and wrong.

In the hallway she heard Em's voice. "I thought I heard her scream, Ruel."

"Oh, my God, Em!" Ruel sighed angrily. "She saw a lizard and it frightened her. I heard her cry out, too. That's why I . . . Oh, what the hell!"

Both their footsteps retreated down the hallway and Julie didn't hear any more of their conversation. She cried—for what she'd done and what she'd lost. It was a long time before the well went dry. She lay on the bed in a stupor of pain after it was over.

She knew she couldn't hide in her room forever. Sooner or later she would have to face the others. Struggling out of the coverlet, she walked to the bathroom and scrubbed her reddened and swollen face. From the closet, she took her long house robe and put it on, zipping it all the way to her throat. Then taking the hairbrush, she began raking it through her tangled hair with punishing force.

There was a knock at the door and she froze. "Wh-Who is it?"

"It's me, Emily. May I come in?" This time she waited for permission before entering.

If only she'd done that the last time, Julie wished sadly. At least the results wouldn't have been so humiliating. Heat flooded her cheeks as she turned away from the door.

"Come in," she said.

When the door opened, Julie didn't turn around. She continued to brush her hair, stroke after stroke. She heard Emily step in and close the door. She kept her back turned to the woman.

"I want you to know, Julie," Emily began quietly, "that coming here is very painful to me, as painful as it is to you. But it's important that we have this talk."

"I quite understand why you're here," Julie admitted, and lowered the brush. She closed a hand around the bristles, letting them dig into her palm. The physical pain was preferable to Emily's gentleness.

"I did cause you a great deal of embarrassment by walking in like I did. For that, I apologize. However, you must know that I will not tolerate a repetition of this afternoon."

"Yes," Julie nodded, "I guessed that would be how you felt. You needn't worry about asking me to leave. I'm willing to give you my resignation and forfeit whatever salary I have coming. I'll leave tonight if you wish."

"Leave? I don't want you to leave, Julie," Emily protested. "That was never my intention."

"Please." Julie turned, trying to salvage some of her pride. "I know what you must think of me and——"

"I think you're a human being, capable of moments of weakness," Emily Harmon interrupted. "I don't condemn you for what happened, but neither will I condone it."

"I don't expect you to." Julie crimsoned, her gaze falling away under the directness of Emily's.

"My nephew is a handsome, virile man—I've been aware of that for a long time. You're a young, beautiful woman, so it's perfectly natural for an attraction to spring up between you. Unfortunately I can't permit this affair to continue."

"Yes, Ruel has already mentioned that he doesn't generally become involved with hired help." A hint of self-pity crept into her biting reply.

"Hired help? I don't consider you hired help, Julie," the older woman sounded indignant. "You seem practically a member of the family to me. Whatever faults I may have, I never have looked down on anyone because they worked for someone."

"I'm sorry, Emily."

With a sigh, Julie replaced the hairbrush on the dressing table and walked to the French doors. The gauzelike sheer panels cast a film over the courtyard, darkening with the twilight shadows.

"I seem to be making a mess of this," Emily sighed. "I think I do understand what happened here, Julie. Ruel is a charming and persuasive individual when he chooses to be."

"Oh, please!" Julie whirled around in protest. "Regardless of what he told you, Ruel isn't the only one to blame for what happened. I was a very willing participant."

"I didn't mean to suggest that he was forcing himself on you or seducing you against your will. I believe I'm aware that your desires were mutual."

"They were." Embarrassment rouged Julie's cheeks even as she admitted the truth.

"I hope you don't think that I've reached the age of fifty-nine without having experienced the heat of passion. I do know what it's like to be carried away by my emotions," Emily said with gentle patience. "I never married, but that doesn't mean I was never in love."

"I know it doesn't," Julie murmured.

"My lover was stationed here in the military. I lived for those hours when he was off duty and could get a pass to see me. The world seemed perfect when I was in his arms. The moments we stole to be together were the most precious." There was a beautifully poignant quality to her voice. "When he left, he promised he would come back to me, and I believed him."

"What happened?" Julie's own pain was put aside for a moment, replaced by compassion for the woman who had become like a friend to her.

A rueful smile twisted Emily's mouth. "He went back to Georgia and married his high school sweetheart."

"I'm sorry, Emily."

"It was all a very long time ago and has little bearing on today." Emily shrugged off the sympathy, primly squaring her shoulders. "You and Ruel are adults. If you feel strongly about each other, I can't prevent it. If you wish to see each other, if you wish to go out on dates, I can't stop you—I wouldn't even try. You would have my blessing. But I will not permit the two of you to carry on an intimate relationship in this house."

"I promise you it will never happen again," Julie vowed.

"You do understand why? I have Debbie to consider. She's sixteen, not yet an adult and I want to instill in her a sense of values, a respect for herself as well as others. How she decides to live when she's on her own is beyond my control, but in the meantime, I can control her home environment and I will."

A tightness gripped Julie's throat. She was reminded again of how very fond Emily was of her niece. The woman was so selfless in her love that Julie's admiration for her knew no bounds.

"So you understand, Julie, I didn't come here to embarrass you by bringing up what happened. I care about you too much to ever deliberately attempt to humiliate you. But I wanted to make it clear to you why I disapproved so strongly about what happened. I'm not a prude. I simply love my niece," Emily concluded with touching simplicity.

"And I know she loves you, too, Emily." It was a surprise to discover a slight welling of tears in her eyes. Julie had thought they were all gone.

"In that case, why don't you get dressed and join me for dinner?" Emily suggested. "It's five minutes after seven and Malia will think no one is coming for dinner."

Not twenty minutes ago Julie had not cared whether she ever had another meal again. The thought of eating would have made her gag. Now, after being subjected to Emily's healing gentleness, the idea was not unpleasant.

"It will only take me a few minutes to dress and I'll be right down," she promised.

"I'll give you exactly five minutes to dress before Malia starts serving," was the warning.

Julie believed she meant it. Emily always meant what she said—that was one of the good things about her. People always knew where they stood.

The private discussion had eliminated any chance of strain between the two women. Their dinner was typical of many they had shared together over the last months. Afterward Malia reminded Julie that she had not been in to see Debbie yet, so she corrected the omission.

"Hi!" Her cheerfulness was fairly genuine as she entered Debbie's bedroom. A wheelchair occupied a corner of the room. "It won't be long before you start joining us for dinner in the evenings."

"I think I've forgotten what it's like to eat at a table. Auntie Em will have to teach me my manners all over again," the girl joked.

"How'd all the tests and X-rays go at the hospital?"

Debbie's answer was a long and detailed one, colored with incidents with doctors and interns and nurses. In quick summary, she concluded that she was progressing faster than the doctors had thought she would.

"That's great," Julie smiled.

Keen dark eyes gave her a long look. "Have you

been crying? Your eyes look a little bloodshot, Julie."

"I went swimming this afternoon. Maybe the chlorine in the pool irritated them." Julie didn't exactly lie; she avoided the answer.

"I sure would like to know what's going on around this place," Debbie sighed. "First Malia tells me you'll be in to see me before dinner, then Emily comes in to say you have a headache and aren't feeling well. You're in your room and may not be down for dinner. Now you say you went swimming."

"What's so strange about that?" Julie asked. "I could have gone swimming, got too much sun, had a headache, didn't feel well and lay down for awhile. Now I'm better."

"Yes, which is why Ruel went slamming through the house before he left, shouting in whispers at Aunt Em. And it was something about you."

"Oh?" Julie edged away from the bed, turning at right angles to the girl. "What did you hear him say about me?"

"Something about coming back early to talk to you and warning Em about something. I couldn't understand it all. What was it about? Did you have another fight? What does Aunt Em have to do with it?" Her curiosity was almost more than Debbie could contain.

"I didn't have any argument with your brother," she could answer quite truthfully. "I don't know any more than you do what he might have been talking about."

"Why don't you trust me, Julie?" Debbie sighed.

"I trust you," she laughed, but with a hint of reserve. "You've had a long day, better get some rest."

After exchanging good-nights, Julie returned to the living room where Emily was reading. She sat on the sofa and glanced through a magazine. The more she thought about Debbie's comment that Ruel planned to come back early, the more she wasn't ready to see him. She discovered a yellow streak of cowardice running down her back.

"If you don't mind, Emily, I think I'll go to bed. I'm tired," Julie straightened to her feet.

"Ruel said he would be home in another hour or two. He wanted to speak to you," Emily said. "Perhaps you should wait up for him."

"No." Julie refused with a decisive shake of her head. "I'd rather not see him tonight."

"Is that what you want me to tell him?" Emily studied her thoughtfully.

"It's the truth. Besides, I'm tired. It's been an emotionally tiring day." Julie answered. "And I don't think I could cope with a discussion tonight with Ruel."

"I understand," the other woman smiled and nodded. "The morning is soon enough, when the mind is rested and the wits are clear."

CHAPTER TWELVE

A ROSY DAWN crept softly into the bedroom. Slowly Julie raised her lashes to study the sunrise pinking her room. Pushing aside the covers, she climbed out of bed. It looked like a beautiful morning and she didn't feel like missing it. As she started toward the French doors, she saw a piece of paper had been slipped under the door.

Bending down, she picked it up. It was a note addressed to her. She unfolded it and read the bold handwriting: "Julie—Come riding with me this morning. 9.30 in front of the house. Ruel."

She stared at it, reading the message again. It seemed a cold, impersonal thing. Folding it up, she fingered the crease. She wanted more time to think before she met him. The yellow streak down her back hadn't gone away overnight.

Today was Saturday. Julie walked to her closet and took out a pair of jeans and a blouse. She slipped into her bikini, put the clothes over it and folded a clean beach towel to put in her beach bag.

She walked to the French doors and opened them. There was no one in the courtyard below and no sound of anyone stirring in the house. Stealthily and quietly, she made her way along the *lanai* to the stairs.

Reaching the circular driveway, she hurried down the private lane. She didn't pause to admire the panoramic view of the coastline as she made her descent of the switchback. When she reached the junction with the highway, the bus that passed Waimea Bay was just approaching. She waved to the driver to stop, climbed aboard and swung breathlessly into a seat.

The beach was deserted at that early morning hour and Julie had it all to herself. A mould of volcanic rock rose from the sand at the water's edge and jutted into the bay. The rock was often used as a diving board by the more brave and daring swimmers. But Julie wanted only a place to sit and think. With her beach towel as a cushion, she settled onto a ledge.

In the sheltered bay, the gentle waves caressed the shore like adoring slaves. The air was soft and pure, warmed by the steadily rising sun and stirred by the breath of the lazy tradewinds. Behind the bay rose the proud cliffs that had seen the first white man land on the island.

Losing herself in the silent reverie of nature's beauty, it was some time before Julie turned her thoughts inward. Emily would be at the breakfast table on the *lanai* about now. She had sometimes left before breakfast on Saturdays before so Emily would find nothing amiss in her absence.

Ruel would be expecting her to go riding with him, but Julie wasn't prepared to face him yet. She wondered what his opinion was of her, after what happened yesterday. True, he had defended her and taken the blame for what happened. But she kept wondering how he regarded her—desired her, but was that the only basis for their relationship? Yesterday that had been enough for her. Today? Sighing, Julie didn't think she knew.

Laughing, shouting voices came from the beach, and she turned to see a family wading and splashing into the water. Sunbathers were scattered along the golden strand of beach. She was no longer the sole occupant of the scene. A pair of adventurous boys were clambering over the mound of cinder rock toward her.

Standing, she gathered her beach towel and bag and vacated the natural diving platform. On the beach, she walked to an open area of sand and lay out her towel, then stripping down to her swimsuit, she went for a short dip in the warm waters of the bay. When she emerged from the sea she stretched out on the towel to let the sun dry her.

Someone came trotting across the sand toward her, but she didn't bother to open her eyes. Someone was always running across the sand—swimmers, children, joggers. She felt no curiosity to identify who was who.

"California? Julie! I thought I recognized you, but I wasn't sure." Frank stopped beside her, his hands at his sides. His expression hovered between a gladness to see her and an accusation of betrayal.

"Hello, Frank. What are you doing here?" Sitting up, Julie brushed the sand from her palms in an attempt at nonchalance. She hadn't seen Frank since that night at the restaurant with Ruel.

"I stop at this beach every weekend looking for you," he answered. "You didn't come last Sunday.

What happened? Did you and Chandler have such a big night that you slept all the next day? Or didn't you come because he forbade it?" he taunted bitterly.

"Stop it, Frank." Her voice was low and stiff with control.

"Where's the big man today?" he jeered.

"Last week you told Ruel that he didn't own me," Julie reminded him, her brown eyes flashing with amber caution lights. "Well, neither do you, Frank. So maybe you'd just better leave. Take your surfboard and go cool off somewhere."

"Oh, Julie!" His sigh seemed to drain away his bitter anger as he sank to his knees on the sand beside her. "I guess it's pretty obvious I was jealous. When I saw you at the restaurant, I wanted to go berserk."

"I didn't know you worked there," she offered in the way of an apology.

"I guessed that after I saw Chandler. Or at least, I didn't think you would come there with him deliberately, knowing how I felt about you," Frank qualified. "All along I've been thinking you were my girl. I didn't realize he was beating my time. What were you doing going out with him?" Instead of anger, this time there was hurt.

"He asked me to have dinner with him, and I accepted." She locked her hands around her knees and studied the position.

"But why?"

"Because I wanted to accept," she admitted. "I wanted to have dinner with him."

"It must be really convenient, both of you living in the same house and all," Frank breathed in disgust. "Whenever Chandler gets bored, he simply looks to you to be entertained for a while."

"It's not like that at all." Was it? Julie whitened at the thought.

"Why didn't you come last Sunday?" His dark eyes mirrored the rejection he felt.

"Probably because I knew this would happen and I didn't want to discuss Ruel with you. And I don't want to discuss him with you now." Unclasping her hands, Julie lay back on the towel and closed her eyes. She hoped he would take the hint and drop the subject.

"Don't you think I have the right to an explanation?" Frank questioned in a righteous tone.

"No. We're just friends, Frank," she insisted.

"We're a little more than that," he protested. "You're my California girl—everybody knows that."

"I'm not your girl." She kept her voice even.

"Are you *his* girl?" he accused.

A twisting stab of pain went through her, poignant and sharp. "I'm not anybody's girl. And I told you I didn't want to discuss Ruel," she snapped.

"What happened? Has he dropped you already?" Frank jeered.

"Frank!" Opening her eyes, she shot him a warning look.

"Okay, we won't talk about him," he agreed grudgingly, his dark brows drawing together in a furrow of irritation. "If that's what you want, we'll forget about him."

"That's what I want." But Julie knew it was impossible. She would never forget about Ruel. He was embedded too deeply in her mind—and heart.

Frank scooped up some sand and sifted it through his fingers. "One of my buddies is having a *luau* tonight." He shifted his position to sit cross-legged on the ground. "It's going to be a big bash, with roast pig and everything. It should be fun."

"It sounds like it. Are you going?" Julie deliberately phrased it to exclude herself.

"I'm supposed to work tonight."

"Too bad," she murmured in indifferent sympathy.

"I hadn't planned to go," Frank paused. "But I could always call in sick at work. What I'm trying to say is . . . I'd like to take you to the *luau* with me."

"I don't think it would be a good idea," she refused.

"It will be fun, you'll see," he coaxed. "We'll have a good time."

"No, Frank."

"You'll change your mind before the day is over." He wouldn't accept her answer. "Once you get into the spirit of things, we'll have a ball. We can spend the day together swimming and playing in the sand."

He grabbed a handful of sand and held it over her stomach, letting it trickle from his fist into her belly button. Julie wasn't amused. She impatiently brushed the grains off her stomach.

"Will you stop it?" she demanded.

A looming shadow darkened her skin. In the same second, Frank was being hauled to his feet, his tanned face mottled with outrage

"Who do you think you are, pushing people around like that?" Frank was having difficulty getting his balance, like a young, inexperienced bull trying to charge his adversary and unable to get his feet to work.

Ruel's look dismissed the challenge as being of little significance and he turned grim faced to Julie. "You're coming with me," he ordered.

"No, she's not!" Frank shouted, and attempted to throw himself between them.

In a fluid move Ruel pivoted and swung, casually ridding himself of an annoying pest. Frank's forward impetus carried him right into the hooking fist. It all happened before Julie could break the paralysis of surprise and do something to stop it.

"No!" she protested too late. The blow knocked Frank backward onto the beach. Fearing he was hurt, Julie wanted to go to his aid. "Frank——"

Her intention went no farther than calling his name and making a move toward him before Ruel had a steel grip on her arm and was pulling her away. She tried to tug free.

"I said you're coming with me." Ignoring her useless struggles, Ruel reached down and scooped up her beach bag and towel.

"Let me go! He's hurt!" She pried at the steel trap

of his fingers. Frank lay gasping on the ground, unable to move.

"He isn't hurt." Ruel flicked a merciless glance at his victim and began pulling Julie away from the scene. "Except for a bruised jaw."

His long strides were eating up the ground, while Julie continued to balk at being dragged along. His arrogant and callous behavior incensed her.

"If you don't let me go, I'll scream," she threatened, her voice trembling in fury.

Ruel stopped and pulled her around to face him. The ruthless set of his features matched the ominous glint of his narrowed blue eyes. He held her fast, his fingers digging into the soft flesh of her arm.

"If you open your mouth one more time, I'll club you over the head and drag you off by your hair," he told her, the words growling out through clenched teeth.

"You wouldn't dare!" Julie breathed, but she almost believed he would.

Turning her around, he gave her a shove forward. "Get in the car."

The black sports car was directly in front of her. His shove had sent her stumbling toward it. She recovered her balance the last couple of steps to walk stiff-necked to the passenger door. Ruel was there to unlock it and toss her things behind the seat. When Julie was inside, he shut the door and walked around to the driver's side.

His anger was almost a tangible thing, but Julie was a match for his. She remembered the release he had used the last time to vent his wrath.

"Is this going to be another one of your high-speed rides?" she challenged.

He sliced a quelling glance to her and started the car. Like a caged beast, the car prowled onto the highway at a restrained pace. The power of the motor was never called upon to exert its thrust as they traveled sedately over the road. The towering grass of sugar cane closed around them, the red dirt road tunneling a path through the field. At a wide spot, Ruel drove the car to one side and stopped. A touch of a button sent the electric windows rolling down to let the tradewinds blow fresh air through the car.

When he turned off the motor, Julie could hear the wind swishing through the tall leaves of the sugar cane, swaying the mauve tassels on top. Ruel leaned an elbow on the steering wheel and rubbed his mouth, staring resolutely ahead.

"That was completely uncalled for." Julie broke the silence, unable to hold back all the things she wanted to say any longer. "You didn't have to hit Frank."

His hand slammed itself against the steering wheel. "What did you expect me to do?" he exploded, turning the harsh glitter of his gaze on her. "You knew I wanted to see you! I left you a note asking you to come riding with me this morning. And don't tell me you didn't get it, because I slipped it under your door last night. This morning it was on your dressing table. I found it myself when I went looking for you."

"You had no right to be in my room," she

snapped since she couldn't say that she hadn't seen the note.

"We'll discuss what my rights are where you're concerned later on," Ruel promised in an ominous tone. "When I didn't find you in your room, I went looking for you. How do you think I felt when I saw you lying half-naked on the beach with that damned love-starved surfer mooning over you!"

"I don't see why that should upset you," Julie retorted with a haughty tilt of her chin.

"You crazy little *wahine*!" With the swiftness of an uncoiling spring, he seized her shoulders and shook her hard. "It upsets me because I love you!" he declared viciously. At the shocked look that spread over her face, the swayed grimness left his face. The strength in his features was gentled. "I love you," he repeated.

He sought her lips with unerring accuracy, crushing their sweetness against her teeth. All her doubt evaporated under the demanding possession of his mouth. The knowledge seared through her like a golden flame. Somehow her arms found their way around his neck as she arched her body to him. The steering wheel kept interfering with their efforts to be close.

"Damn!" he cursed it as he sought the hollow of her throat.

Frustration welled within Julie, too, at the unsatisfactory embrace. She longed to mould her body to his hard shape, to feel the driving pressure of his thighs grinding against hers. Her breasts swelled under his cupping hand, but she arched from the incompleteness. Finally Ruel lifted his head and tucked her shoulder under his arm, groaning softly as he kissed the corner of her eye.

"I never guessed . . . " Julie twisted sideways, tipping her head back to see his face and sliding her fingers inside the buttoned front of his shirt to feel his hair-roughened skin and the pounding beat of his heart. "I didn't know you loved me," she told him.

The invitation of her parted lips was one he couldn't resist. His kiss was hard and brief, keeping the fires of passion burning, but not letting them blaze out of control.

"I told you I did yesterday." His glowing look seemed to radiate over her. "Don't you remember?"

"No." She wouldn't have forgotten something as important as that, not even in the deafening heat of the moment. "Unless—you said something in Hawaiian."

"*Aloha auia oe.* I love you," he translated. "*Ku'uipo,* my sweetheart, my lover."

He brushed his mouth over her lips. His hand fitted itself to the curve of her neck, his thumb rubbing the hollow under her ear in a sensual caress. Julie quivered under the spell of his potent charm.

"I would have made sure you understood me yesterday," Ruel told her. "Unfortunately Em walked in." His jaw tightened in remembrance. "It tore my guts out to see you in that ball of misery and shamed embarrassment. I knew how humiliating it was for you. That's why I was so harsh with Em, and myself. I wanted to comfort you, to convince you that it would be all right. But as long as Em was there I knew you wouldn't listen to anything I said. She wouldn't leave for fear I would revert to my lusting ways. And I had that damned appointment. I was caught between a rock and a hard pole."

"It all worked out, though," she reassured him, reaching out to trace the outline of that formidable mouth with her fingertips. The clean, male smell of him was an aphrodisiac to her senses.

"But it was hell in the meantime." He exhaled a long shuddering breath.

"It's heaven now." It had been a remarkable and swift transition from the depths to the heights.

Her head was tipped far back on his shoulder. With a grown, Ruel covered her lips. His hand slipped across her bare stomacn to grasp her rib cag and attempt to turn her into his arms, but the hard curve of the steering wheel blocked them again.

"Dammit, Julie," he muttered against her cheek, "why didn't you wait up for me last night? We could have had this whole thing straightened out by now and in more comfortable quarters. I broke every record getting back, only to find you'd gone to bed I would have awakened you, but Em would have taken the cane to me. But this morning—why didn't you meet me this morning?"

"Because I didn't think I could face you, so I ran," she admitted. "I didn't run very far from you. I didn't want to, not until I'd made up my mind."

"About what?" He molded his hand to her breast and seemed enchanted with its shape. His erotic touch was building the flames again, the heat spreading to other areas.

"Until I'd made up my mind whether I could handle it when you became bored with me."

"Bored with you!" Ruel leaned his head back against the seat and laughed at the ceiling. "That's been the problem since the beginning. I've never been bored with you. Not from the moment you came down the stairs that first morning, looking as if you owned the place. You walked across the room to me, as bold as you pleased, and looked me right straight in the eye."

"You'd been talking about the Kona winds." Julie remembered it as vividly as he obviously did that precious first meeting. "And you knew who I was immediately."

"You weren't a bit impressed with my deductive prowess," Ruel accused. "In fact, you prodded me into telling you who I was, blithely admitted you were lost and asked directions. You were the most fascinating and intelligent creature I'd met in years."

"Was I?" she marveled.

"As if you didn't know," he mocked. "Running around with flowers in your hair, chasing after fires, and dangling your surfer under my nose."

"I didn't do that," Julie denied the last.

"Whether it was deliberate or not, you succeeded in first arousing my envy and finally my jealousy." A light lurking in the depths of his eyes warned Julie not to do it again.

"Were you really jealous of Frank?" She knew he had never had any reason to be.

"A lot of females get turned on by those young,

muscled bodies balanced on a surfboard," Ruel answered.

Her hand spread over the solid muscles of his chest to the firmness of his stomach. "I haven't found anything wrong with your body. It's tanned and hard and warm."

"Damn you, Julie!" He closed his fingers over her hand. "You keep that up and you'll find out just how warm and hard it is. This car isn't designed for making love."

"No?" She felt a sense of power in being able to arouse him and exercised a little of it now.

"No," he repeated firmly, but his gaze wandered down to the swelling curves of her breasts, exposed by the cut of her bikini top. Julie felt the shallowness of his breathing. "I want to make my intimate discoveries of you at a more leisurely pace and in a more comfortable place. So don't you wave temptation in my face."

"No?" Provocatively Julie peered at him through her lashes.

Roughly he twined his fingers into her hair, holding her head still while he punished her lips. The hard, shattering kiss went of control. Ruel was parting her lips, deeply exploring and engulfing her mouth.

A horn honked, loudly, as a truck rumbled to a squealing halt. It honked again in blaring demand as Ruel surfaced with shuddering effort. Shaken, Julie could only lean weakly against him.

"Hey, boss! It mo' betta if you move dat car!" a

male voice shouted in local pidgin. "We gonna fire dis field *wikiwiki.*"

With a saluting wave of his hand, Ruel acknowledged the advice and information. He set Julie completely in her own seat and reached behind it for her beach bag.

"Here." He put it in her lap. "Get some clothes on before you lose those you've got."

The cane truck squeezed past them as Ruel started the car. Fighting the cramped quarters of the front seat, Julie managed to pull her jeans on and shrug into her blouse. When the truck was behind them. Ruel reversed the car and maneuvered it back the way they had come.

"Was this where we were going to come when we went riding?" Julie asked as they emerged from the dirt road to the drive. "Here to watch the cane field burn?"

"Probably." He slowed the car to a crawl. "I just wanted to get you away from the house where we could talk. Which reminds me. . . . " He reached out to take her hand.

"What does?" Julie asked.

Ruel turned to study her. "I've been the one who's done all the talking."

"And?" She was puzzled by the intensity of his gaze.

"And I think it's about time you did some talking," he challenged.

"About what?" she frowned.

A truck rumbled up behind them, its horn blaring. There wasn't enough room for it to pass. Ruel swore under his breath and waved his arm out the window for the truck to wait.

"Hey, boss! Have you gone *pupule?* You can't park dat car in da road." It was the same driver as before.

"Dammit, Al!" Ruel leaned his head out the window to shout at the man. "I'm not moving until this woman admits she loves me! So lay off that damned horn!" Impatience was in his expression when he looked at her. "Well?"

That was what he had been waiting for her to say. Julie laughed in delight. She thought she had told him a hundred times—a thousand times.

"I love you, Ruel Chandler," she declared in a buoyant voice.

"It's about time you said it." His gruffness was the most beautiful sound she had ever heard, as his hand cupped the back of her head to draw her mouth to his.

In the truck behind them, the driver laid on the horn, announcing to the world the answer she had given. It became the second most beautiful sound she'd heard.

Back by Popular Demand

Janet Dailey
Americana

A romantic tour of America through fifty favorite Harlequin Presents, each set in a different state researched by Janet and her husband, Bill. A journey of a lifetime in one cherished collection.

In August, don't miss the exciting states featured in:

Title #13 — ILLINOIS
The Lyon's Share

#14 — INDIANA
The Indy Man

Available wherever
Harlequin books are sold.

THIS JULY, HARLEQUIN OFFERS YOU THE PERFECT SUMMER READ!

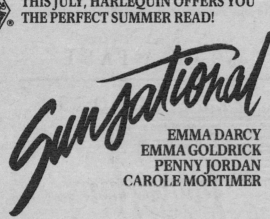

EMMA DARCY
EMMA GOLDRICK
PENNY JORDAN
CAROLE MORTIMER

From top authors of Harlequin Presents comes HARLEQUIN SUNSATIONAL, a four-stories-in-one book with 768 pages of romantic reading.

Written by such prolific Harlequin authors as Emma Darcy, Emma Goldrick, Penny Jordan and Carole Mortimer, HARLEQUIN SUNSATIONAL is the perfect summer companion to take along to the beach, cottage, on your dream destination or just for reading at home in the warm sunshine!

Don't miss this unique reading opportunity.

Available wherever Harlequin books are sold.

This October, Harlequin offers you a second
two-in-one collection of romances

A SPECIAL
SOMETHING

THE FOREVER
INSTINCT

by the award-winning author,

Now, two of Barbara Delinsky's most loved books are
available together in this special edition that new and
longtime fans will want to add to their bookshelves.

Let Barbara Delinsky double your reading pleasure with
her memorable love stories, A SPECIAL SOMETHING and
THE FOREVER INSTINCT.

Available wherever Harlequin books are sold.

PENNY JORDAN

Sins and infidelities...
Dreams and obsessions...
Shattering secrets
unfold in...

THE HIDDEN YEARS

SAGE — stunning, sensual and vibrant, she spent a lifetime distancing herself from a past too painful to confront... the mother who seemed to hold her at bay, the father who resented her and the heartache of unfulfilled love. To the world, Sage was independent and invulnerable— but it was a mask she cultivated to hide a desperation she herself couldn't quite understand... until an unforeseen turn of events drew her into the discovery of the hidden years, finally allowing Sage to open her heart to a passion denied for so long.

The Hidden Years—a compelling novel of truth and passion that will unlock the heart and soul of every woman.

AVAILABLE IN OCTOBER!
Watch for your opportunity to complete your Penny Jordan set.
POWER PLAY and SILVER will also be available in October.